HER CHANCE AT *Love*

NICKI NIGHT

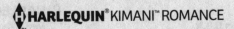
HARLEQUIN® KIMANI™ ROMANCE

Recycling programs
for this product may
not exist in your area.

ISBN-13: 978-0-373-86428-7

Her Chance at Love

Copyright © 2015 by Renee Daniel Flagler

HARLEQUIN®
www.Harlequin.com

Printed in U.S.A.

Nicki Night is an edgy hopeless romantic who enjoys creating stories of love and new possibilities. Nicki has a penchant for adventure and is currently working on penning her next romantic escapade. Nicki resides in the city where dreams are made of, but occasionally travels to her treasured seaside hideaway to write in seclusion. She enjoys hearing from readers and can be contacted on Facebook, through her website at nickinight.com, or via email at nickinightwrites@gmail.com.

Books by Nicki Night

Harlequin Kimani Romance

Her Chance at Love

Visit the Author Profile page at
Harlequin.com for more titles.

This book is dedicated to my shero, Eva Daniel,
who is now cooking with the angels.

Acknowledgments

A few years ago, I attended my very first RT Booklovers Convention
and was determined to return one day as a romance author on the
other side of that signing table. By the time I left my hotel, story
ideas for handsome heroes and spirited heroines were pouring into
my soul. It was as if a portal had opened up! My author-girlfriend
Zuri Day gave me an amazing boost of confidence,
and when she told me, "You can certainly do this!"
I then took my ideas, the gift that God had blessed me with,
and my laptop and started writing.

In 2014, I returned to RT Booklovers Convention armed with
proposals, trained pitches and juicy tidbits about the stories that
flowed through me. You could only faintly—very faintly—imagine
my absolute delight when Glenda Howard suggested that I email
her my proposal and the first three chapters of my story. Now I'm
here…writing acknowledgments for my very first romance novel.

There's a long list of folks that I want to thank for being
instrumental in this journey, starting with God. Father, I give You
ALL the glory! Zuri Day, you sassy Caribbean Queen, thank you
for your vote of confidence. Glenda Howard, thank you for taking
a chance on a girl from Queens with big dreams. Brenda Jackson,
thank you for your friendship and for imparting so much wisdom
on me during our lively lunches! Tony Dunlop ESQ, thanks
for helping me keep the legal aspects of this story authentic.
Donna Hill, my friend, my romance idol, thank you for taking
the time to read my baby and for giving it your stamp of approval.
To Harlequin's entire Kimani Romance team, thank you for your
role in bringing *Her Chance at Love* to life. To the love of my life,
Les, and my entire family, thank you for sharing me with my
passion and believing that I can accomplish any crazy thing I set out
to do. To the book clubs and readers, thank you for embracing me!

To everyone, as my bestie, Renee Daniel Flagler, would say,
"Always #DreamEnormously!"

Ciao darlings!

Your friend,

Nicki

Chapter 1

"You haven't had sex in how long?" Alana Tate shrieked.

Cadence Payne recoiled as her eyes darted around the bustling coffeehouse and then landed on the shocked wide-eyed expression on her closest friend's face. She couldn't believe how loud she had just said that. "Alana!" she chided, embarrassed for both of them.

"Don't Alana me!" she said, still speaking at the same volume that she had just used to let everyone in proximity know that Cadence hadn't had any in a while. "What are you waiting for? Please don't tell me you're still pining over that loser Kenny. I thought you were over him!" she said, referring to Cadence's ex-fiancé, Kenneth Dalton. "I still can't believe he married that woman so soon after you two broke off the engagement. Jerk."

"Shh!" Cadence waved her hand at Alana, urging her to lower her voice before the entire coffeehouse ended up knowing all her business. "It has nothing to do with Kenny," she found herself whispering, then rolled her eyes and sighed. She knew Alana meant well, but she needed to reel her in before she went too far. Shaking her head, she took a sip of her chai latte. "I just haven't found anyone that I'm interested in dating, let alone sleeping with."

"That's because for the past six months you've dated your job. With the time you've put into working, there's no room for anything else." Alana gave her a pitiful look. "You need to get out more."

"Well, once I make senior counsel, then maybe I'll have time for a date or two." *Yeah, right.* She hoped her statement would be enough to get Alana off her back—even if she didn't believe it herself. Cadence was hurt when Kenny abruptly ended their engagement. Not only did the breakup severely bruise her ego, but also she didn't know love could hurt so badly. Then Kenny poured salt into her already wounded heart when he married another woman a few short weeks after. Cadence stood, indicating that it was time to go. Grabbing her empty cup, she started for the trash can, and then headed for the door. Cadence wanted to get out of that place and away from their topic as quickly as possible, adding distance between her and the notion of dating anyone. Alana was fast on her heels.

"You're coming with me tonight!" Alana declared.

Cadence suddenly stopped walking, causing Alana to crash into her from behind. Clucking her teeth, she shook her head and started walking again. "Where are you going now?" she asked, digging in her oversize purse in search of her car keys.

"The NYAA mixer."

Cadence spun around with her hands up in protest, "No!"

Alana took in a breath and exhaled. "I know you don't like those kinds of gatherings, but you need to get out and meet some new people."

Ignoring Alana, Cadence clicked the car alarm and slid

into the driver's seat. Alana sat next to her, on the passenger's side. The last place she wanted to meet someone was at a mixer full of pretentious lawyers. They reminded her of high-profile cattle calls where arrogant men waltzed around in their tailored suits trying to one-up each other with their dossier of accomplishments, while the women shamelessly put their pedigrees and other things on display for all to see. Her last ill-fated relationship was with a lawyer. Needless to say, that was not a match made in anybody's heaven.

Cadence never did fare well at these types of events. A self-proclaimed horrible networker, she shied away from them as much as she could, which is why she never joined the New York Association of Attorneys. She didn't feel comfortable in the presence of these groups. Besides being somewhat of a loner, she was also the daughter of a senator and had experienced more than her share of inauthentic relationships. Now she just tried to avoid them at all costs.

Without another word, Cadence pulled off and headed back toward her home in Garden City.

"Cadence!" Alana yelled, turning toward her in the passenger seat. "I know you hear me talking to you. It will be fun. We don't have to stay long. Besides, I'm on the board of the local chapter, so I have to at least show my face."

"No, Alana! I'm not going."

Alana grunted. "You really should give it a try. I've made so many great connections."

"I have all the connections I need. My dad is a senator, remember?"

"Your own connections…" Frustrated, Alana shook her head. "Besides, it will be good for you to meet some of the members and see how we do things. You really should consider joining. You'd be a great addition."

"I'm doing fine on my own. You know social groups aren't my thing."

"It's a professional organization, not some social club." Alana blew out an irritated breath. "Well, you owe me anyway! Come tonight and we can call it even."

Cadence nearly slammed on the brakes. "Owe you for what?"

"Dragging me to your annoying cousin's party."

"Oh…that." Cadence sighed, casting her eyes sideways. She had to admit, that event was a disaster. She'd felt obligated to attend because it was family but didn't want to go alone, so she'd lugged Alana along with her promising that she'd make it up to her.

"So, yeah. You owe me." Alana smiled, sitting up in her seat as if she'd just won a prize.

Cadence cut her eyes. "I still didn't say I was going." Alana turned toward Cadence and stared.

Cadence's resolve collapsed as she pulled the car to a park in front of Alana's condominium. "Okay. I'll go."

"Yay—" Cadence cut Alana's celebration off with a narrowed eye and a pointed finger. "What?" Alana drew the inquiry out.

"I'm not staying more than an hour. So when I've had enough, you have to leave with me."

"Trust me. You'll have a blast." Alana leaned over and hugged her friend. "I'm driving, so I'll pick you up at six. We have to get to midtown before seven and I want to be sure to get a close parking spot."

Cadence looked at the green digital numbers illuminating the dashboard. "It's five thirty now! I have to get home, shower and find something to wear."

"See you at six," Alana reiterated with a huge smile, ignoring Cadence's alarmed expression as she exited the car. "I have to get there early. Trust me, you won't be disappointed." She slammed the door and then leaned over, gesturing for Cadence to roll down the window. Sticking her head in, she said, "Now that I'm getting you out, the next thing we need to do is get you a man so you can get laid." Alana howled at Cadence's twisted lips. Cadence rolled the window up on her and pulled off, watching Alana continue to laugh through her rearview mirror.

Chapter 2

Blake Barrington looked at his brothers and shook his head. Both Hunter's and Drew's backs were bent as they held their stomachs, roaring at Blake's expense. At first, Blake tried not to be taken in by their antics, but couldn't help himself and eventually folded and let loose his own contained laughter.

That was the third woman in the past fifteen minutes that had practically thrown herself at Blake's feet. He wondered if his brothers were trying to prank him and actually ran his hand across his back as high as he could to make sure they hadn't posted any crazy signs. The last woman was the weirdest of all, approaching him by taking his hand in hers and kissing the back side. When she lifted her eyes to meet his, Blake wasn't sure if the dark shading over her lip was moisture from a drink or a real-life mustache. However, when he looked down at the spirally coils springing from her ample cleavage, he realized his vision wasn't failing him. From the looks of it, this woman had a robust supply of testosterone. Instinctively, his hand went to his chest and he thought about the fact that she had more hair on hers that he did on his.

"Enough already," he chided his brothers, who continued to laugh uncontrollably. Drew's eyes glistened and he fell into a coughing fit. Hunter had to pound him on the back a few times. Blake shook his head and called the waitress over and ordered another round.

When Drew was able to regain his composure, he straightened his back, wiped his tears and breathed deep. "Sorry, bro. I couldn't help myself. Your Sasquatch radar is obviously on the blink. I wish you could have seen your own eyes when they landed on her mustache." Drew fell into another fit of laughter.

"Don't worry, man—" Hunter placed a reassuring hand on Blake's shoulder "—big brother will show you how it's done," he said, picking up the snifter of whiskey the voluptuous barmaid had just placed on the counter. Passing one glass to each brother, he said, "Cheers," and lifted the blend in the air for a toast before throwing back a healthy sip.

They had met at the trendy lounge early enough to share a drink together before the NYAA mixer started. Hunter and Blake had followed their father's example of becoming attorneys. At twenty-nine, Hunter was the oldest with Blake trailing him by eleven months. Drew, the baby of the crew, was two years Blake's junior and the rebel of the family. Despite acquiring his JD, he opted to pursue his passion in the world of motorcycles instead of practicing law. His championship races and award-winning designs graced the pages of the most popular motorcycling-enthusiast magazines.

Taking notice of the growing crowd, Blake looked at his watch. Throwing back his last sip of whiskey, he winced at the favorable burn and placed the glass back down on the bar. "We should get going." Blake led the brothers through the dimly lit lounge down to the lower level, where the mixer was actually taking place.

Nodding at a few familiar faces along the way, Blake narrowed his eyes in search of other members of the board. He had recently been elected as a director on the executive board to replace his predecessor, who had just resigned due to relocating. Their father had always told them to be sure to rub elbows with the right people. It certainly helped him become a judge. After taking in the scene and surveying the women, Blake took a seat next to his brothers at the bar.

"Who's that?" Drew's eyes were stretched wide. Blake's and Hunter's eyes followed his line of sight. When they noticed whom Drew was inquiring about, simultaneously they reared their heads back.

"Stay away from her. Ask Blake," Hunter said.

"Her name is Mandy, and it took me six months to get her to stop randomly showing up at my door with lingerie on under an overcoat."

Drew raised his brow. "You must have really put it on her," he said, smiling and resting his back against the bar.

"Actually, no. I was dating her friend and she had obviously shared a few details with her about our...eh... encounters. Once we stopped dating, that's when Mandy started showing up talking about how much she'd heard about me and wanted to experience a few things for herself." Blake angled his back toward Mandy, who seemed to be walking in their direction.

"Is she a lawyer, too?" Drew asked.

"Yeah, but she just joined the organization," Hunter added.

"Wow. All those brains and she's still crazy. Ha!" Drew slapped his leg at his own remark.

"Yeah. That's why I've sworn off dating other lawyers.

It's not cool sleeping with a woman and the next morning you find yourself sitting on the opposite side of the negotiation table and your clients are at war with each other," Blake said, thinking of a similar encounter with the last attorney he dated.

"That's just awkward," Drew said, raising a brow.

"Yeah. And it's happened more than once," Hunter added.

"Whoa!" Drew raised his fist to his mouth as the brothers joined together in laughter once again.

"Hey, Blake." Alana rose on her toes to give Hunter a friendly hug before turning to his brother. "Hey, Hunter, Drew," she acknowledged, and hugged them, too.

After Alana's greeting, Blake zoned out. Well, it wasn't entirely his fault. It was the goddess who stood immediately behind Alana that had captured his attention and momentarily rendered him deaf and mute.

Alana reached behind herself and pulled the woman to her side. If she hadn't looked so disinterested, Blake would have made his intentions clear right then and there, but, sensing her attitude, he decided he'd let things play out before making his move.

Shaking his head, Blake jumped back into the conversation. He was almost annoyed with himself at how he'd let a single look at this beautiful woman throw him off guard.

"What did you say your name was?" he asked the woman, holding his hand out to shake hers. A bland smile spread across her beautiful heart-shaped lips—one that told him she really wasn't interested in being here. Despite the lack of enthusiasm, she managed to spark a rise in him that he hadn't expected.

"Cadence Payne."

Her soft voice caressed Blake's ear ever so slightly, giving rise to several parts of him, as if she'd teased him with an actual touch. Blake was caught in the sheer femininity of it. It actually took him a moment to respond. "Beautiful name. Pleasure to meet you, Cadence." Blake brought the back of her hand to his lips and kissed it gently and then flashed what he hoped was a winning sexy smile potent enough to put a dent in that attitude of hers.

"Pleasure," she said dryly, and pulled her hand back.

This one had a hard exterior, Blake concluded. He wasn't worried about that. He'd never had a problem breaking through women's exteriors before, no matter how tough they tried to be. Women often melted under the Barrington brothers' influence. The brothers were hot commodities, and had even been featured in a special issue of one of the local magazines as some of the most eligible bachelors in the greater metropolitan area.

"So, how has it been going so far? Has our speaker arrived?" Alana asked, rising to her toes to look over the crowd.

"Not that I know of," Blake responded, still looking at Cadence, who had been trying to avoid his stare.

"Okay. I'll check it out. Be right back." Before Blake or Hunter could reply, Alana was off through the crowd, mingling, smiling and waving at familiar faces in the distance.

Instead of following her, Cadence took a seat at the far end of the bar. Blake took her aloof demeanor as a sign to let her be for just a while, but there was no way he was going to let her leave there without getting her number.

"Are you done?" Drew said as he and Hunter grinned.

"Huh?" Blake said, realizing their eyes were on him awaiting a response. "What?"

"He asked, 'are you done?'" Hunter yelled over the noise of the growing crowd.

"What do you mean?"

"Are you done lapping her up with your eyes, man?" Drew laughed. "She doesn't seem interested."

"What?" Blake grunted. "Not interested in me!" He

feigned surprise as if Drew's assessment was completely ridiculous. "Dude, do you know who I am?" he asked, touching his chest in disbelief. "I'm Blake Barrington! You better ask around," he teased. Hunter and Drew dismissed him with waves of their hands.

"Well, she doesn't seem to care," Drew responded. "Seems like she's got a bit of an attitude anyway. Do you know if she's an attorney also?"

"I know she is," Hunter answered.

Blake's head spun in his brother's direction based on his response. "You know her?" He wondered what he may have missed during the introductions when he had been arrested by her pouty lips, nice hips, caramel skin, perfect breasts and long legs.

"You know her, too," Hunter said, holding his finger up at the bartender for another round. He nodded, confirming her acknowledgment before turning his attention back to Blake. "That's Senator Payne's daughter. I've never actually met her up close and personal, but I know that face."

Blake's shoulders slumped in disappointment upon finding out that she was also an attorney. He'd been serious when he'd vowed to stop dating women in the same profession. It never worked out for him. He even wondered how he'd never run into her before. New York City was a crowded metropolis, but many of its circles ran small.

"Hey!" The high-pitched shriek snatched his attention away from his thoughts about Cadence.

Before he could fully turn himself around, he felt the softness of a woman's body pressed up against the back of him. The familiar, sweet essence of lilies wafted from Jasmine Lee's almond skin. He found himself smothered in her arms as she closed them tightly around him.

"What's up, baby?" Jasmine said, turning him around, grabbing him by his cheeks and then pulling him down to her—right into her full, indulgent baby-pink lips.

The unexpected interaction put him on Pause and he found himself wondering if Cadence had been watching. Jasmine was a brazen flirt, and he'd already made up his mind to give Cadence time to unwind before he zeroed in on her. Jasmine's greeting could affect his chance of getting closer to Cadence.

Blake pulled away, but Jasmine grabbed his hand, which he retracted as politely as possible. Hunter was carrying on the conversation. After her overbearing greeting, Blake had yet to focus on a single word that she'd said, though his eyes were involuntarily drawn to all of the cleavage that had been stuffed inside her pink blouse.

"I need to take care of a few things. I'll see you around, Jasmine," he said, taking his chance to escape, leaving Jasmine to his brothers. He went in search of Alana to get some details on her friend before making his move.

Blake was stopped several times as he tried to snake his way through the thick crowd in an unsuccessful attempt to locate Alana. Several minutes later, the music lowered and lights flickered on, brightening the room. Blake turned in the direction where Don Shaver, the president of NYAA, had just cleared his throat to welcome the guests and began to introduce the board members in attendance. Blake made his way to that side of the room, temporarily aborting his mission. He'd have to obtain details on Cadence later. When his name was called as the newest addition to the board, he pasted on his most charming smile and stepped in line with his fellow board members.

Once the introductions had been made, the officers blended back into the crowd as Don introduced the speaker for the night, who happened to be Blake's mentor, Congressman William Banks. By this time, the crowd was so thick Blake couldn't find Alana. Making it back over to where his brothers were posted at the bar, he looked over Drew's shoulder in search of Cadence and found her gone.

Congressman Banks's voice boomed over the crowd and he recited an anecdote that Blake had heard many times. Sighing, Blake realized he wouldn't accomplish his mission of making a move on Cadence this night. He wanted to hear whatever his mentor had to say but would be sure to find Alana and get the details on Ms. Cadence later.

Chapter 3

Cadence arrived at the office a half hour early, just as she had for the past few months. At twenty-eight, she had her heart set on becoming the company's youngest woman to make partner. Snagging the current open position of senior counsel would put her on track for making that happen in record time. She was putting in all the extra effort that was necessary to secure this promotion. Even though she wasn't much of a people person, she made a concerted effort to be more engaged with her coworkers.

As early as it was, her eyes were already strained and tired from going over documentation from the case she was working on. Cadence placed her palms on her cherrywood desk and pushed herself up. As she stood, she brushed off the front of her pin-striped slacks, heaved a deep breath and headed through the desolate office toward the break room.

Popping a French vanilla K-Cup into the coffeemaker, she leaned back against the counter as she listened to the machine hiss against the quiet backdrop of the empty office. Cadence crossed her arms over her chest and recounted the items on her task list. Her latest case was a doozy. Not so much because of legal aspects. *That* she could handle. The client, on the other hand, was a handful.

Richard McLennan was a young spoiled rich brat that never knew a day of hard work in his life. He was unsuitably left to run an accounting firm he'd inherited as a result of his father's sudden death. Recently, he'd been doling out sexual harassment settlements like federal income tax payouts after April 15. Cadence, along with the company's board, had been advising him to focus on the business rather than his employees' "assets." Unfortunately, the young know-it-all was convinced he had everything under control, despite the new claims being filed on a weekly basis. Cadence knew that if the media caught wind of this fiasco, the company would suffer a serious blow to its image.

The hiss of the coffee machine settled as the last drops of brew gurgled into Cadence's mug, capturing her attention. Adding French vanilla creamer to deepen the flavor, she closed her eyes and sniffed, taking in the rich aroma. Just as she was about to take a much-desired sip, Kerry Cooper's nasal voice sliced right through her indulgent moment.

"Morning, Cadence," Kerry purred like a slick feline. Cadence's stomach contracted and she discreetly rolled her eyes.

Standing straighter, Cadence spread her lips into a tight smile and turned to face her colleague. "Good morning to you, Kerry," she said with what she'd hoped came across as a polite nod of her head.

Kerry pranced into the break room, sporting a sly smile, and stepped dangerously close to Cadence before grabbing a K-Cup of her own. "Guess who I had dinner with last night?" Kerry sang.

Who cares? "Who?" Cadence asked, immediately taking a sip of her scorching coffee in an effort to hide the scowl that threatened to take hold of her lips.

"Richard McLennan." Kerry raised her brows as if dropping the name gave her a big win.

Cadence paused mid-sip, feeling heat rise from her belly. *Did you sleep with him, too?* Instead of the curt words she wanted to say, she opted for something a little less cheeky. "He seems like your type." Cadence tilted her head and smiled pleasantly, enjoying the questioning look and narrowed eyes glaring back at her. Though her head was filled with questions and she felt like a knife had been lodged in her back, she refused to let Kerry get a rise out of her. "Chat with you later," she said cheerfully. Exiting with a glide, she could feel Kerry's eyes boring into her back.

Once she got into her office, she dialed Alana on her cell phone.

"Do you know what that woman did this time?" she poured into the phone without giving Alana a chance to say hello.

"It's too early for this. Hold on and let me close my office door." The line went silent for a moment and Cadence could hear the door shut. "Okay. I'm back. What on earth happened?"

"She had dinner with my client!"

"Shut the front door! Isn't that a conflict of interest?"

"Not necessarily. As long as nothing substantive about the case was being discussed, there's no problem with it. You know that."

"Well, it should be."

"I know, but it's not like she'd admit to anything anyway. She's clearly up to something. Ever since she found out that I was also in the running for senior counsel, she's been slithering around this office trying to rile me up one way or another. I don't trust her as far as I could throw her." Cadence paced circles around her desk.

"How did you find out?"

"She just told me." Cadence pivoted, her breathing escalated with every step. She plopped down on the front of her desk and took a deep breath. "You should have seen the devious smile on her face."

"Who else was there?"

"Just us."

"And what did you say?"

"That he seemed like her type, and I sauntered my behind out of the room with a winning smile." Cadence chuckled.

"Ha! That's right, my lady. Never let 'em see you sweat! Sounds like you could probably use a drink after work. Why don't you meet me in that lounge over by Seventh and Twenty-Third?"

Cadence frowned. She really could use the drink, the company and a dose of her best friend's humor, but when she thought about how much work she had ahead of her, she knew she'd have to decline. Reasons for saying yes and no volleyed in her mind.

"Come on! I can tell by your silence that you're probably thinking of an excuse to tell me why you can't come. We all have a lot on our plates," Alana said as if she had read Cadence's mind. "We all need a break sometimes, Cay. Come let down your hair. I won't keep you out too late."

What else could she tell her? "Aw, what the hell! I'll be there."

Alana's piercing squeal caused Cadence to pull the phone away from her ear. "I promise it will make you feel a little better." Cadence shook her head, chuckling at her friend. "Oh. I forgot to tell you," Alana said. "I'm meeting a few folks from the organization there, also. They'll arrive around seven. We have to hash out some details for our next mixer. You and I can meet right after work so that by the time they show up, if you want to head home, you can, but you are more than welcome to stick around. It shouldn't take long for us to handle our business. Please don't say you won't come because of that." Cadence could hear the pleading in Alana's voice.

"Okay." She dragged the word, stretching out the response. "See you at six."

"Yeah!" Alana squealed again.

Cadence cringed and then she heard a light tapping at her office door. "I gotta run. See you later," she whispered into the receiver.

"Blake will be there," Alana added just before she disconnected.

Cadence acted as if she hadn't heard what Alana said, but her core tightened slightly at the mention of Blake's name. "Come in," she caroled, rounding her desk as she headed back to her chair.

Adam Benjamin, her direct boss and one of the partners whom she held in high esteem, stuck his head in her door. "Morning, Cadence."

Cadence stood, offering a polite nod and smile. "Morning, Mr. Benjamin."

Adam looked behind himself before entering her office completely as if he was sneaking around. "I just want to say you're doing a great job. Keep up the good work." He clasped his hands. "You never know who's watching." His friendly smile warmed the atmosphere.

Cadence dipped her head. "Thank you, sir. I'll keep that in mind." Out of all of the partners at the firm, Adam had always managed to make Cadence feel welcome, in a sincere and professional kind of way. Had the decision of making her senior counsel been solely up to him, she would have had the position already. Unfortunately, it took more than Adam's approval.

Cadence should have been elated about Adam's surprise drop-in. Despite the enlightening fact that he had let her know she was on their radar, she couldn't keep her mind from slipping back to what Alana had said before she ended their call. "Blake will be there." *Why would Alana say that? Why should I care?* She had to admit to herself that despite his apparent arrogance and obvious playboy ways, he was absolutely gorgeous.

Cadence saw him staring at her from across the bar the other night, but when all those women—beautiful, voluptuous and ultrathin women—continued to pour all over him, she decided she probably wasn't his type. She found herself a corner and stayed holed up in it until Alana was ready to go.

"*Blake will be there.*" Alana's voice replayed in her head and tingling sensations that had long since become unfamiliar to her came rushing back with fervor. She felt like a teen with a secret crush—one that would have to remain undisclosed. He was an attorney. She remembered her vow to stay away from his kind. Furthermore, with her limited dating history, she wasn't equipped to handle a real-life playboy. She needed to keep her heart at a safe distance.

Chapter 4

When Cadence finally looked up at the clock, it was well past two in the afternoon. She blinked and moved her eyes toward the glass clock on her desk. She hadn't moved from her chair in hours. Twisting her head, Cadence tried to work out the kinks that had settled in her neck and shoulders. Then she stood, raising her arms over her head for a quick stretch.

"Come in," she said in response to the urgent rapping at her office door.

The nervous look on the office assistant's face caused the kinks that she had just worked out to stiffen in her shoulders. "Uh…Cadence…we have an—" Amy Fisher's mouth formed as if she was going to say *issue*, but before she could get it out, Richard McLennan came stumbling through Cadence's office door.

Immediately, Cadence was on her feet. Before she could catch herself, she'd released an audible gasp at the sight of her disheveled client. If his reddened complexion and tousled hair didn't leave her questioning what the heck was going on, then the huge shiner adorning his right eye certainly raised its own barrage of questions.

"Richard!"

"Cad…" Richard cleared his throat as he staggered toward her. "Cadence! I want that tramp arrested!"

Cadence quickly rounded her desk, catching Richard just before he fell into the back of a chair.

"Richard! Look at me," Cadence ordered, wiggling his chin to get him to look directly at her.

His focus wandered aimlessly as he tried to talk. "She socked me right in the eye!" The words tumbled out of his mouth before he hiccuped. "I'm suing her for every dime she's got," Richard slurred, and Cadence's senses were assaulted by the strong odor of coffee and whiskey that permeated the air around him. She assumed he'd started his day with a couple of hot toddies.

"Amy, get him a cup of black coffee and meet me in the conference room." Cadence snaked her arm under Richard's and guided him out of her office through a sea of inquisitive stares from coworkers, and into the conference room. Richard, a crumpled mess, had been mumbling all along the way.

Once she successfully planted his sinewy body in a chair, Cadence took a deep breath, once again taking in the sharp odor of whiskey that wafted from his mouth. She paced a few times as she tried to gather herself before asking her next set of questions. She couldn't believe what she was witnessing.

Amy scurried into the room with a steaming cup of black coffee and tried to get Richard to drink some. His head bobbed as if he had no control of his neck. Amy had to support his chin to get his mouth to the rim. Tipping the cup, she got him to swallow a few sips before placing it down on the sturdy mahogany table.

Cadence sent Amy to get Adam so she would have another attorney in the room before she began asking Richard questions. She was at least thankful that he'd begun to calm down a little. He had stopped mumbling incoherently and was now drinking the coffee on his own.

Cadence jerked when Richard slammed the cup against the conference table. "I need another cup!" he barked.

Amy was just about to enter the room, but instead nodded at Cadence, exiting swiftly toward the break room.

"What's going on here?" Adam's voice bellowed as he entered the room. Rearing his head back at the sight of the large purple-and-black ring surrounding Richard's eye, Adam looked back and forth between Cadence and Richard. "What the hell happened?"

"That tramp." Richard cleared his throat. "She socked me in the eye."

"Tell me who and why," Adam said.

Cadence stood next to Richard, arms crossed, awaiting his answer.

"Victoria Kelly!" Richard said, slamming his hand against the table and then flashing a look as if he thought this was ridiculous.

Cadence closed her eyes, shook her head and sighed, recognizing the name as one of the employees that had filed a recent sexual harassment claim against him. "Tell me exactly what happened, Richard," she said calmly, taking a seat next to him.

Adam shook his head and sat, also. Once again, Cadence tried her best to keep her composure and remain stoically professional as Richard gave an absurd account of how he'd simply brushed against the backside of an employee from whom he'd been warned to keep his distance. In addition, as he said, one thing led to another and, before he knew it, she'd wound up her arm and unleashed a blow that connected directly to his right eye. After that, he ran out of the office, jumped in a taxi and headed straight to the law firm.

"When I get back to that office, I'm going to fire her so fast!"

"Okay. Rich. Calm down." Cadence was speaking softly while her eyes were on Adam, whose brows were still tightly knit as he nodded his head. "How about you get some rest and I'll take care of everything." Cadence was sure his claim wouldn't hold water in light of all of the recent filings against him, but her job was to try to do all she could for her client. Right now she needed to get him calm and sober.

"I'll call for a taxi. Go home and get some rest, and then after that we can get started filing your claim."

"Whew!" Richard held his forehead. "Thanks, Cadence. I knew you would handle it."

"Cadence always does," Adam added proudly. Cadence smiled for the first time since Richard came barreling into her office.

"Don't go back to the office today, okay, Richard? If you need anything, I'll have Amy call and have your secretary send it to your house.

"That won't work." Richard threw his hands up in the air.

"Why not?" Cadence looked confused.

"Victoria is my secretary, remember?"

"No worries, Rich. We'll see that you get what you need." Cadence assured him.

Just then, Amy walked back in with another cup of coffee. Richard, finally settled, took the cup, nodded halfheartedly before he began drinking.

Adam got up from the table and patted Richard's back. "You're in good hands, Rich. Take it easy and we'll get everything under control."

Rich simply nodded.

"Cadence, can I speak to you for a moment?" Adam motioned for Cadence to follow him into the hallway. Adam looked back in the room before speaking. "You need to get to the bottom of this right away. Once you're sure he's home and settled, get over to that office and see how far this has gone. See what you can find out. We need to handle this as quickly and quietly as possible."

"Yes, sir."

Adam cast her a hopeful glance before heading back to his office. Cadence watched his long legs sweep across the floor in quick strides as she avoided going back into the conference room for just a few more minutes. She took a deep breath, dropped her shoulders and straightened her back, bracing herself for the task at hand.

There was no telling how this would all play out. She knew that meeting Alana for drinks after work wasn't likely to happen. Alana would understand. What Cadence found surprisingly disappointing was the fact that she wouldn't get to see Blake tonight. Even if she knew she wasn't his type.

This new fiasco with Richard would eat up a considerable amount of Cadence's time. The progress she'd made earlier in the day would mean nothing now that she had to shift her focus and try to clean up his latest mess. She made sure he'd made it home safely before she prepared for the trip to his company to get answers.

The display on her cell phone lit up as it shimmied around her desktop. She'd put off calling Alana to cancel their plans for the evening long enough. Cadence sighed and picked up the phone.

"Hey, girl," Cadence said.

"What's the problem now?" Her lackluster greeting apparently put Alana on alert.

"I can't even begin to tell you. My sleazebag client managed to dig himself an even deeper hole. I won't be able to meet you tonight."

"Aw, Cadence!"

"I know. I'm so sorry, but there's nothing I can do about it. I'll make it up to you. I promise."

"Okay. Duty calls. Handle your business, *chica*! We'll catch up."

"Thanks! Now I'm off to clean up this sleazebag's—I mean, my client's—mess."

"Wow, is that how we address our most valuable clients these days? I wonder if the partners would take issue with that."

Cadence's head popped up at the sound of Kerry's voice, which sounded more like fingernails on a chalkboard.

Cadence bit back what she really wanted to say. "Eavesdropping, are we?" Cadence replied and forced a smile.

"You need to let me at her one of these days," Cadence heard Alana say as she held the phone to her ear.

Cadence smiled on the inside, remaining cordial and professional on the outside for Kerry's benefit.

Despite the fact that Cadence was still obviously on the phone, Kerry sauntered the rest of the way into her office and planted herself on the edge of the desk. Silent moments passed as Cadence stared at Kerry, taken by her rudeness. Kerry tinkered with the picture frames on her desk.

Another beat passed. "Can I give you a call back?" she asked Alana politely.

"Getting the picture," Alana obliged. "Handle your business, my friend. We can chat later."

"How can I help you, Kerry?" Cadence asked.

Fingering figure eights along the desktop, Kerry took a moment to respond. "I see that your client has gone rogue."

"I guess you can say that." Cadence busied herself gathering the documents that she'd pulled together for her visit to Richard's office. "But soon it will all be under control." She stood, hoping Kerry would get the hint and leave her office.

"Perhaps I could help," Kerry offered.

Cadence smiled, once again biting back the words she preferred to say. "I think I can handle this on my own."

Kerry pouted. "Oh. That's too bad. I figured you'd appreciate my assistance." She slid down from Cadence's desk. "I thought you were a team player," she said as she sauntered toward the door. "It would be a shame if the partners got the impression that you weren't." Slowly, she turned away, tossing the words "Good luck" over her shoulder.

Standing rigid, Cadence felt her insides grow warm. She fought to keep her cool. Kerry was always able to get under her skin, but she refused to let it show. Closing her office door, Cadence took several deep breaths to rein in her temper. Then she reasoned with herself that Kerry was just trying to rattle her competition and, although she could probably acquire some dirt on her, she vowed to earn a clean win, allowing her merit and work ethic to garner the position she coveted. She wasn't going to fall prey to Kerry's ways. Then she remembered that Kerry had bragged about hanging out with Richard the night before, which made her wonder if she had anything to do with what happened at his office today. Shaking off the anxiety brought on by those thoughts, Cadence stuffed her documents into her bag and moseyed through the office with her head held high.

Meeting Alana and seeing Blake would have been a great way to cap such a disastrous day, but unfortunately, that would have to wait. Right now she had business to take care of and a position to fight for. This was another testament to the fact that she had no room in her life for dating anyway.

Chapter 5

Blake had successfully proved that he was a jack-of-all-trades as he helped get things set up for the mentoring organization's annual career fair. The organizers seemed technically inept and after several attempts to hook the computers up to the university's Wi-Fi system, he jumped in and saved the day.

Blake and a few other NYAA members had volunteered their Saturday to help young high school and college students with their résumés. Now that the laptops were set up and most of the folks who'd signed up to help out had arrived, it was almost time to tackle the long line of students waiting to get their résumés evaluated and typed.

From the looks of things, they weren't going to be leaving anytime soon. He had to call on some members to bring in additional recruits. Alana had promised that she would rally a few extra hands on her own. The fruit of her labor was yet to be seen as Blake anxiously awaited her arrival, hoping she'd bring at least five more volunteers with her.

What he really wanted to know, but didn't dare ask Alana during their phone conversation, was if her friend Cadence would be coming along. He still hadn't had a chance to work his charm on her but couldn't seem to get her off his mind. Despite the fact that this volunteer effort would offer him little time to focus on wooing Cadence, he was determined to make some kind of move. He refused to let her get away again without at least getting her number.

"Blake!" Sandy Grove, one of the other volunteers, yelled. "This thing is not printing."

Blake trotted over to the station where they had set up several printers. "Let me see," he said, checking all the connections. "Everything looks good over here, Sandy. Did you make sure that you selected the right printer?"

"What?"

Blake shook his head at the sheepish grin she flashed at him. "You have to go into the control panel and add the one you want. Did you do that?"

"No! I figured after all of that tinkering you did, it would just happen." She snickered.

Blake chuckled. "Scoot over," he said, gently shoving her to the side." Blake tapped on the keys for a few seconds. The copier clicked and the document came sliding out. "There you go."

"Blake, you're cute *and* smart!" Sandy giggled.

"Gee. Thanks, Sandy," Blake said sarcastically and shook his head at her.

"Now, don't get a big ego," she said, nudging him on the arm.

"Blake!" someone else called from across the room. He dropped his head.

"You're being summoned again." Sandy sang and laughed once more.

"Coming." Blake jogged in the direction of the call.

This time, the organizer needed him to help another vendor set up.

When Blake was done, he looked across the room, hoping the backup volunteers had arrived. The fair would be opening in minutes and the lines were now snaking around the corner, as he was told. The vendor thanked him and he shot back across the university's gymnasium to the other side.

Alana had arrived, and as she'd said, she had seriously rallied the troops. She had at least ten more volunteers with her.

"Alana!" Blake leaned in and wrapped her in a grateful hug.

"Did I do well?" she asked, presenting the folks she brought along with a sweeping gesture.

"You did very well." Blake was especially appreciative of the fact that she'd brought Cadence along. Blake waved a general greeting to the group but kept his eye on Cadence, flashing his most brilliant smile. "Welcome and thanks, everyone. Just give me a moment and we will get you all set up as fast as we can. Did you all bring laptops?" The crowd collectively affirmed by nodding their heads. Some lifted their laptops in the air. "Great." Blake clapped his hands together, but before he could show them where they needed to be, he heard his name being called again through the PA system.

The frenzy had heightened. With minutes left, representatives from recruitment companies, other businesses and vendors lined the perimeter of the gymnasium, scurrying to prepare their tables for the throngs of students outside of the double doors.

Blake helped yet another vendor gain access to the university's Wi-Fi, showed the organizer how to do it for the umpteenth time and headed back to make sure his group was ready to go.

While he was gone, Alana had taken charge finalizing the setup. She had the custodians pull out a few more tables. A total of five six-foot-long tables were lined up in two rows with three volunteers set up at each table. She had also set up table signs that said, Résumé Services Sponsored by the NYAA.

"Let's do a test run to make sure all of you are connected to the printer correctly." Alana stood addressing their group as if she were conducting a symphony.

"Thanks, Alana!" Blake pulled her into another friendly hug.

"You know I've got your back. Everybody printing okay?" Alana asked.

"I'm getting an error message." Cadence said.

Before Alana could respond, Blake had run to her side. "Let me help you out." Once again, with a few clicks, he had her all set up and her test page was sliding out of one of the printers set up behind them.

Blake trotted over to retrieve the printed page and brought it back to her. "There you go," he said, making a point to graze her hand as he handed it to her. The slight touch sent heat surging through him. He seized her with his eyes and allowed his gaze to linger. Cadence turned away first, but not before Blake made his point. He could tell by the slow way she dipped her eyes that he'd affected her, too.

As Blake walked away, he couldn't help the quick groan that escaped his throat. He had to remind himself to remain focused, though it would be hard, since he still smelled the sweet scent of her perfume, which now permeated his nostrils. He wished he could capture the way it mixed with her scent and recall it at his will.

Blake looked at his watch. The doors would be opening in less than a minute. "Okay. Is everyone up and running?" The group responded with a collective yes. "Great! We are ready to go."

Seconds later, the doors opened and students from all backgrounds poured into the gym, filling the space with their wide-eyed excitement. Immediately, all fifteen volunteers were busy helping to proofread, evaluate and rewrite résumés and offer career advice in response to the many questions the eager students asked.

It was quickly determined who served best in certain capacities, and the group made the necessary adjustments to keep the flow of traffic moving. Alana's hands moved like lightning across the keyboard. She and a few others who typed fast focused on retyping résumés that required major editing. Cadence and Blake were really good at helping the students put their skills into words. They began to help those students who needed assistance with sprucing up their job descriptions.

With so many people seeking their help, the morning blazed by. Blake hadn't realized how hungry he was until his stomach growled right in the middle of telling a young woman how to reword her administrative skills. Her endearing eyes bore into him the entire time he spoke and she smiled sheepishly when it was time for her to speak. When they were done, he typed in the last of her changes, printed the résumé and bid her good luck with a professional handshake.

As much as he loved the attention from women, he was never one to take advantage of a young starry-eyed girl. Politely he sent her on her way. As she made her way around to the vendors' tables, she kept looking back at him.

His stomach growled again, reminding him that it was time to eat. He stood before another student took the seat in front of him. "You guys hungry?"

"Yes" rang out at various pitches.

"We can take turns going to get something to eat or I can just run and grab something for all of us." Blake looked out over the line of folks that never seemed to cease. "Things don't seem to be slowing down anytime soon. How about I go get something for all of us? I could use some fresh air."

"That's probably the best idea," Alana confirmed.

"So what do you say? Pizza? Sandwiches?"

"Pizza is probably easiest," Cadence said.

When she spoke, it was like music to Blake's ears. He agreed just because she made the suggestion. "Pizza it is!" he said before anyone else could offer any other suggestion. "I'll grab a couple of pies with a few different toppings." Blake paused a moment, not wanting to seem too anxious. "Cadence, would you like to ride with me? I could use some help picking toppings."

Cadence seemed to stiffen. It took a moment for her to respond. Alana's back straightened and she turned to see how Cadence would answer. When she finally said yes, Blake realized that he'd been holding his breath.

Chapter 6

Cadence needed Blake to help her climb into his big shiny pickup truck. He handled her so gently she had to tighten her body to keep it from shivering under his touch. She almost couldn't believe that she had agreed to go with him. Maybe it was because the side of him that she'd witnessed today made her want to get to know him better—even if she didn't think she was his type. She noticed the special attention he paid to her—the way he held her hand just a bit longer than necessary, the way he softened his tone when he addressed her and the fact that she constantly caught him stealing glances at her.

Before today, Cadence pegged him as just another arrogant lawyer—a *gorgeous* arrogant lawyer. After watching him in action helping out the organizers and working so diligently with the students, she started to draw new conclusions about him. It took a special person to even volunteer time for a cause such as this. She loved the way he always seemed to have everything under control.

Now Cadence allowed her eyes to follow him as he rounded the truck, after helping her in like a gentleman. As she watched him, she recalled eyeing his beautifully masculine hands as they skillfully moved across the keyboard as he typed out résumés. She remembered the way the muscles in his back strained against his shirt when he leaned over to pick up a box of paper to refill printers. The majestic rise of his chest when he stood to talk to people painted a glorious picture in her psyche. Several times she had to force herself to look away and focus on a student or her laptop in an effort to clear her mind of him. She liked the way he operated. All of it was topped off with an incredible dose of swagger that made her want to swoon.

When he climbed in on the driver's side, she turned her head to look out the window. Those visuals continued to flood her mind as she sat next to him in his truck. Being so close to him in such a small space made her skin grow warm on the surface. Shifting in her seat, she almost felt as if she couldn't handle the pressure of sitting near him and having to stare into those dark mysterious eyes of his. Cadence could drown in the abyss of his dimples. She imagined sticking her tongue inside of them. *Where did that thought come from?* It embarrassed her, as if he could hear what she was thinking. Cadence looked down at her fumbling hands and chuckled.

"Did I miss something?" Blake inquired.

"Huh?" *Dang it. Why did he have to speak?* The deep sultry purr of his voice gave her pause. She was so lost in the soothing rumble that she hadn't even heard what he said.

"I thought I heard you laugh. I was wondering if I missed something."

"Oh. No."

A beat passed. Then another. Neither of them moved. Cadence was caught in the smoky gaze he cast her way, hooking her like a fish. Then he smiled again, flashing pearly-white teeth lined up in a neat row framed by full beautiful lips. Blake licked his lips, and his smiled curled up on one side. The sexy grin woke up feelings in Cadence that she thought she buried months ago. His dimples sank into his cheeks and once again she felt the urge to stick her tongue in them.

Cadence cleared her throat and sat up straighter in her seat before looking around the interior of the vehicle as if she was taking it all in. "Big truck you have here." She closed her eyes. Those words didn't sound right. She tried to think of something else to say. "I wouldn't have pictured you in a truck like this."

Blake sniffed out a small laugh. "What makes you say that?" he asked as he put the pickup into gear and backed out of his snug parking spot.

"I don't know. I just figured you'd be more of a luxury-car kind of guy."

"Judging me, are you?" he teased.

"No. Not at all."

Blake grinned. "I can't fit my bikes into those cars."

"You ride?" Cadence asked, and regretted the words the second they came out of her mouth.

Instead of answering right away, Blake let her question simmer, looking as if he was trying to suppress a naughty grin. "Why? Do you like riding…" He let his partial inquiry hang in the air. "Bikes?" he finally added.

"Blake!" Cadence called him on the innuendo and they both burst out laughing.

"You set yourself up for that one," Blake said, still laughing.

"I realized that." Cadence shook her head. Now that his focus was on the road they swiftly covered, she could steal glances. She paid special attention to the lines of his profile, the neat edge of his goatee and the jut of his strong chin.

"To answer your question, yes. I really enjoy my bikes."

"Wow! *Bikes* as in plural, huh?"

"Yeah! My brothers and I are quite the adventurous types. We usually use my truck to haul our bikes, ATVs, Jet Skis, you know. Right now I've got my eye on a cruiser."

Cadence wasn't quite sure what he meant by a cruiser but just assumed it was another type of motorcycle. Those things were excessively dangerous for her liking. She didn't miss the gleam in his eyes as he talked about what appeared to be his favorite pastime.

"You ever ride?"

"No!" she practically sang, shaking her head as if the thought of her riding was completely absurd. "I've never even been on a scooter."

"Maybe I could take you for a ride one day."

"Thanks, but no thanks!"

Blake just laughed. "There's a pizza shop right up here. What should we order?" he asked as he cut a left on Hempstead Turnpike.

"I think three pies should do it. We can do a cheese pizza, one with pepperoni and one with some kind of veggies," Cadence said.

"That's cool. That way, we'll have everyone's tastes covered."

Blake and Cadence continued to make small talk as they ordered and waited for the pies. Once they were back in the truck, a companionable silence settled between them. He managed to get the same prime parking spot next to the entrance of the gymnasium.

Blake turned off the engine, but instead of getting out, he simply sat back. Cadence wondered for a second, trying to figure out why he wasn't moving.

"Cadence."

Dang it! Every time that man called her name, it did something inexplicable to her. "Yes?" Her voice was mousy. She cleared her throat and tried again. "What's up?"

"I'd really like to get your number."

"Really?" Cadence's brows scrunched. She knew she was picking up signs, but she really didn't believe he'd be interested in her for any reasonable length of time. She remembered the sexy women that poured all over him at the mixer. She wasn't interested in casual sex or other meaningless relationships, so why bother wasting either of their time?

"Why do you seem surprised?"

"I...well..." She paused for a moment, getting her thoughts together. She didn't want to come across as harsh. "I've got a lot on my plate right now and..."

"Do you eat?"

"What?"

"You're about to tell me about how you don't have time to go out, but you have to eat, right?"

"Yes." She let the word out slowly, narrowing her eyes at him. She knew where this was going. Blake wasn't taking no for an answer. It was obvious that he was probably used to getting his way with women.

"So don't worry about making time. Just let me treat you to a nice meal."

Cadence released a sound that started like a grunt but ended like a chuckle.

Blake pulled out his phone tapped the screen a few times before speaking again. "You eat on Fridays, right?"

Cadence nodded her head. "Yes. Blake."

"Okay. So wait until about eight o'clock next Friday night to have your dinner. I'll pick you up and bring you right back so you can continue tackling all that stuff you have piled up on this plate you're talking about. Now, what's your number?" he said, holding his phone up, waiting to tap in the information.

Cadence obliged, giving him her number.

"See, that wasn't so hard, was it?" Blake teased. "I'm dialing you so my number will be in your phone. Store it now."

Cadence shook her head again. "You're pushy!" she teased back.

"Come on. Let's get these pizzas inside," Blake said as if he was giving her an order, before trotting to the passenger side to help her out of the truck.

The same tingling sensation that crept across her skin the first time he touched her returned when he took her hand. Cadence slid down, landing in the small space left for her between the car door and Blake's body. At first, Blake didn't move. He kept her there, sandwiched between him and the vehicle. Cadence narrowed her eyes at him and with a sly grin he stepped aside, grabbed the boxes of pizzas from the back and led the way inside.

Cadence knew then that there was no way she'd be able to go to dinner with him next Friday night. There were far too many reasons why she simply shouldn't. Blake was a playboy and an attorney—two things that she tried her best to avoid at all costs. Most important, she wasn't about to be caught up with the type of man who casually ran through women. She'd just have to ignore all of the sensations that managed to belie the best of her virtuous intentions when he was around and save herself the heartache.

Chapter 7

Blake stood and stretched his long lean body toward the ceiling and then twisted his torso from one side to the other. The day was finally coming to a close. He and the other volunteers had just helped the last of the remaining students. His mouth was dry and his wrists were sore from typing for the past nine hours. As he looked around, other volunteers were also stretching, twisting and shaking their limbs after hours of sitting. Vendors were packing up their booths, getting ready to hit the road.

The two slices of pizza he had for lunch had long since worked their way through his system and now his stomach rumbled as if there were a wrestling matching going on inside him. He looked over toward where Alana stood chatting with Cadence and smiled. He found himself wondering what they were talking about. Remembering the time he'd had alone with Cadence earlier made him smile. As tired as he was after such a long day, he didn't want it to end. Actually, he didn't want to see Cadence go. He now had her number and plans for dinner, but with her scent lingering in his nostrils, he decided he hadn't had enough of her for today.

Blake shook his head, not believing his own thoughts. Did he want more of Cadence? That truth intrigued him because he couldn't understand what it was about her that drew him in like a magnet. He was a Barrington brother. They had their pick of women. Many threw themselves at the brothers all the time, so why was it that he couldn't seem to get this one out of his mind?

Since the first day he laid eyes on her, he'd been absorbed by thoughts about her. Cadence seemed like a challenge, but he'd had women who played hard to get before. Unlike the others, he wasn't interested in conquering this one as a challenge just to prove that he could before moving on.

Blake heard his name and turned in time to see the organizer heading his way. He wanted to see what the gentleman had to say, but he didn't want to lose sight of Alana and Cadence.

Jeff shook Blake's hand. "I can't thank you enough for all of your help, man."

Blake nodded. "You're welcome."

"Hey, listen, you and your team were great. I'd like to talk with you more about some of our other programs, maybe pull you in to speak to our students sometime."

"Sounds like a plan." Blake was sincerely interested in hearing more, but as he looked around, he saw that Cadence had packed up her laptop and slipped her purse onto her shoulder. He didn't want her to leave before getting another chance to talk to her. Blake turned his attention back to Jeff. "Send me some information. I'd be happy to work something out."

"Great!" Jeff shook Blake's hand harder, smiling and nodding his head appreciatively.

Blake looked past him and saw Alana and Cadence heading for the door.

"Jeff, I need to run. Shoot me an email and we'll set something up."

Taking off in Cadence's direction, Blake called out her name. He had to repeat it several times over the noise of chatter, packing tape and tables and chairs being dragged across the floor. Catching up with them right at the door, Blake opened his arms and pulled Alana into a bear hug.

"Thanks for always pulling up the rear."

"Oh, Blake, please. You know I always come through."

After squeezing Alana in that friendly embrace, he turned his attention to Cadence. "Thanks for coming with me for the food run earlier."

"Sure." Cadence just smiled and nodded.

"I can't get a hug?" Blake asked, drawing his cheeks down into a pout.

Cadence cast her eyes heavenly, shook her head and stepped into Blake's waiting arms. When Blake fastened his arms around her, he sucked in a delicate whiff of her natural scent mixed with her floral perfume. Instinctively, his eyes closed and his gut tightened. The soft feel of her cool supple skin was almost intoxicating. After letting his embrace linger, he reluctantly pulled himself away. His earlier thought returned. He wanted more of Cadence.

"Let me take you ladies to dinner. It will be a token of my appreciation for all your hard work today. You have to be hungry. I know I'm starving."

"Of course you can take me to dinner! I say no to drugs, not food!" Alana said. They all chuckled before turning their attention toward Cadence, who had yet to respond to Blake's invitation.

Cadence's response was already etched into her face. Blake could see it. His knotted stomach also felt it. "Not to—"

"Come on, Cadence!" Alana cut into her objection before she could get it all out. "You just said you were hungry," Alana blurted. Cadence stretched her eyes at Alana and cut her a sharp glare. Alana dismissed Cadence with a wave and turned her attention to Blake. "Where are we going to eat? She didn't drive, so she's riding with me."

Cadence tossed her hands up in defeat. "I guess I'm going to have dinner with you two." She cut her eyes back toward Alana. "Next time, I'll bring my own car."

Alana smiled and winked at Cadence before turning her attention back to Blake. "Don't mind her. She's just a homebody. Sometimes I have to practically drag her out of the house."

"You like Asian fusion?" Blake directed his question toward Cadence.

"Sure," she said, with mock enthusiasm.

"Let's go to Asia Moon on Franklin," Blake suggested. "It's not too far from here."

"Oh yes!" Alana said. "I could use one of their martinis."

"Okay. Let me grab my stuff and close things out over here. I can meet you there in about—" Blake looked down at his watch and mumbled as he calculated "—twenty minutes?" Blake waited for the two of them to nod their approval before turning and jogging back to the table where his laptop still rested. Thankful for Alana's insistence, he felt like jumping in the air and clicking his heels. Because of her, he'd have another few hours to work his charms on Cadence.

One way or another, he was determined to break through that shell that Cadence had erected around herself. He snickered when he thought scandalously about what he'd find on the inside—all puns intended.

Chapter 8

"Now *you* owe me!" The words shot out of Cadence's mouth like cannonballs. She jammed her seat belt into the slot, sat back and folded her arms.

Alana snickered. Cadence glared at her and Alana fell into a fit of laughter as she maneuvered the car out of the lot. "Stop acting like you don't want to go to dinner with that man—that fine man!" she sang.

"It's really not a big deal."

Alana slammed on the brakes, forcing Cadence's body to jerk forward. "Girl! It's me! Don't sit here and act as if you don't find him attractive. He was all over you today." Alana shook her head, looked both ways and continued driving.

"No, he wasn't." Cadence rolled her eyes, pressing back her smile.

"Please! Cadence wants pizza, we all have to eat pizza," Alana said, waving a hand in sweeping gestures. "Wanna come with me to get the pizza, Cadence?" she said, pulling her voice down a couple of octaves to mimic Blake. "He looked at you like you were his lunch. Let's not even mention the hug before we left. I thought he would never let you go."

Cadence turned her head to face the passenger window so Alana wouldn't see her blush. "You're exaggerating," she finally said, once the burn in her cheeks subsided.

"I don't know why you are playing games. You haven't had a man in over half a year and here comes this tall drink of refreshing spring water, flowing from a crystal glacier. No. Scratch that! A fine specimen, complete with multiple degrees and the body of a god. He's the perfect catch. I can't believe you want to just toss him back in the water like he's some ugly catfish!"

Cadence cut her eyes at Alana's overzealous description of Blake. "If he's so great, then why don't you date him?"

"Blake is off-limits. I used to date his brother," she said matter-of-factly.

"What? You didn't tell me that. Which one?" Cadence didn't hide her surprise. "I thought I knew all of your boyfriends."

"Drew. It wasn't serious. We went out a couple of times."

"Oh." Cadence held her smile on the inside, happy to hear that her friend wouldn't possibly be interested in Blake. "I don't like playboys, and besides, I doubt I'm his type. My boobs aren't large enough to choke me when I lie down, and I don't speak bimbo."

"Ha! Those brothers attract all types. He's a good catch and he gives back to the community. In fact, they all do. That's what I like about them."

"I can see that."

"Blake is very active in this organization that mentors young boys. He's always taking them out and doing things with them. It's really cool. I think it helps to keep him grounded."

Cadence quietly pondered what Alana had just said. She admired people who gave back.

"Plus, he seems to be genuinely interested in you. Just give it a chance. You never know what can happen."

"I don't know. Maybe I'm just not ready to date." She'd gotten over Kenny, but not those feelings of rejection. The last thing she wanted was to get her hopes up about someone who probably didn't take a woman's feelings seriously. He may have been a reasonable humanitarian, but he was still a man who appeared to be a playboy.

"Well, you may not be ready for him, but I know for sure that he's ready to get to know you a little better."

"What makes you say that?" Cadence tilted her head, eager to hear Alana's response.

"Ever since the mixer, he's been asking about you."

"You didn't tell me that." Cadence rose in her seat and then sat back, hoping she didn't appear too anxious.

Alana shrugged as if it was no big deal.

"We're here." Alana peered over the dash to get a better look at the front of the restaurant. "That's it right there. I'm sure there's more parking in the back. I'll pull around." Alana whipped the car into the lot and pulled into the first available spot. "This is probably the closest we are going to get. It looks crowded."

The ladies checked their faces in the visor mirrors and headed inside. Alana stood on her toes, craning her neck over the crowd in search of Blake, while Cadence discreetly scanned the restaurant with her eyes. It didn't appear that Blake had arrived yet.

"Let me see how long the wait is going to be," Alana said.

Cadence followed Alana as she snaked through the thick crowd toward the hostess. Their wait would be about forty-five minutes and the women figured that would work since Blake had yet to arrive.

"Can I take your name?" the young hostess asked Alana.

"Ah." She paused, looking at Cadence for confirmation. Cadence shrugged. "Sure. Alana. Party of three, but our third party is not here yet."

"Okay. You said Alana, right?" the woman asked, and Alana nodded. "Will you be dining with Mr. Barrington this evening?"

Cadence and Alana exchanged surprised glances. "Yes, we will. How'd you know?"

Offering up a pleasant smile, the hostess said, "Oh, Mr. Barrington called ahead, so we were expecting you. Follow me," the hostess said with a nod, grabbing several menus and leading them through the loud bustling restaurant to a room set aside for private events. They were seated at a table for at least eight people and the hostess placed a menu at each setting. Turning to them, she smiled and nodded again. "I'll send your waiter right over. Mr. Barrington and the rest of your party should be with you shortly."

"Thank you," Alana said to the woman politely before turning to Cadence. "How the heck did Blake manage this?" she said, referring to the fact that they were seated immediately despite the long wait.

"I don't know, but I'm glad we don't have to wait the whole forty-five minutes. I thought about leaving but, re-alizing that it's a Saturday evening, every other restaurant will have a similar wait." Cadence couldn't help glancing around as she anticipated Blake's arrival.

"Yeah, but Blake didn't offer to treat us to those res-taurants. Ha!" Alana teased.

"Thanks, Kim," Blake's voice sounded off just outside of the room where Alana and Cadence sat.

Cadence turned around so fast she almost gave herself

whiplash. She hoped Alana hadn't noticed her eagerness because she sure wouldn't let her live it down.

Blake stepped into the room where they were seated with one of his arms extended out to the side. "Ladies!" Several of the other volunteers from the career fair stepped in behind him, looking more like his personal entourage. Taking a seat at the head of the table near Cadence, he smiled wide, rubbing his hands together. "I hope they didn't make you wait long."

"Not at all," Alana spoke up first. "How did you manage that? Those people out there are waiting at least forty-five minutes to be seated."

"Let's just say, I know a guy." Blake's laugh bellowed and bounced off the walls in the enclosed area.

The group exchanged greetings with one another. Cadence was thankful for their presence, assuming it would take the pressure off sitting at the table with Blake. Their waiter showed up immediately and took their orders. Idle chatter about their volunteer work ensued until the food arrived. The crew was so hungry that little was said while they indulged. The noise level at the table grew considerably once the food had been finished and drinks began to flow more frequently.

Cadence enjoyed the cuisine and the company and was almost glad that she hadn't gone straight home. It was a nice departure from her normal routine, though being alone never bothered her. As an only child, she was accustomed to stillness. With tons of work and a voracious love of books, boredom had never been an issue.

Blake brushed across her hand, causing small tremors to travel up her arm. He was holding court but never failed to let her know that he was including her with a touch or glance or by somehow pulling her into the conversation if she appeared to get too quiet. She appreciated his small gestures of inclusion.

As the drinks flowed, the dialogue took on a more animated resonance when the topics changed to relationships. The sharp difference of opinion between the ladies and the men made for an intense debate.

"That's because most men only want one thing!" Sandy practically shouted.

"That's all some women want these days, too." Blake's response generated a collective gasp from the women. "Present company included…obviously," The grumbling response from the women was like a roar. Blake held his hands up. "Wait! Let me say this."

"Let the man speak." Eddie slurred and everyone laughed.

"Being a good-looking man, I come from a different perspective. I come across all kinds of women in my travels. I can take my pick."

"Oh Lord! Will you listen to King Blake," Sandy interjected.

"No!" Blake said, holding his hands up. "Seriously. Even if I wasn't as handsome and dapper…" Blake jokingly paused and posed, offering a gorgeous profile. All three women at the table rolled their eyes simultaneously and laughed aloud. "It still wouldn't matter. Some women are just different these days. They don't have the same values as they used to. As a man, if you don't have your own value system, you could get away with almost anything. If you have more to offer than just your good looks like I do, oh, forget about it! The world could literally be yours."

"I can't believe how arrogant you are." Cadence's thoughts had made it past her lips. Blake was apparently pretty confident about the fact that he was God's gift to women.

"I'm not arrogant, sweetheart. I'm confident. There's a difference." He topped his comment off with a wink.

Cadence hated the fact that his little clarification made

him even sexier and the fact that he'd called her sweetheart made her want to swoon. "Whatever," she said, waving her hand.

"It's true. I'm blessed to have a lot going for me. I'm well educated and I take good care of myself. I try not to get caught up in nonsense and I wish that women out there wouldn't, either. It just clouds the judgment."

"Okay, King Blake. I hate to say it, but you've got a point," Sandy said before raising her glass and taking a sip of her white wine.

"The problem is your delivery!" Sandy cosigned Cadence's comment by shaking her head in Blake's direction.

"Ha! Yeah," Alana added, laughing with the rest of the group. "It makes sense. Some of our women and men do seem to be more concerned with superficial things. At the end of the day, what matters the most is how well you are treated. A person's looks, money or degrees can't hold you at night or tell you how much they love you."

"See!" Blake looked at Cadence. "That's why I could be your ideal man. I'll hold you at night and tell you how much I care—" Blake cast a smoldering gaze in Cadence's direction "—among other things."

A shudder radiated from Cadence's core out to the edges of her skin. Picking up her wineglass, she pushed down the lump that had formed in her throat with a large gulp and hoped no one else caught that.

"If this man toots his own horn one more time..." Sandy threw her hands up in mock frustration.

"I'm with you, Sandy!" Alana added.

"Don't be mad at the truth!" Eddie interjected.

Everyone else at the table was doubled over laughing.

Alana looked at her phone. "Oh my goodness! It's almost nine o'clock!"

"What?" Cadence sat up straight. She had brought loads of work home that she planned to get through. After volunteering earlier and spending the rest of her evening and now most of her night with Blake and Alana, she was sure to get nothing done. She couldn't believe how the hours had passed without warning.

"Wow. How time flies," Sandy said, emptying her most recent refill in one long gulp. Putting the glass down, she placed the palm of her hands on the table and pushed herself up. "This was grand, but I've got to hit the road."

"Me, too," Eddie slurred. Taking a moment to collect his balance he pulled out his wallet. "How much do I owe you?"

"My treat," Blake said, flashing a dazzling smile.

"Thanks!" Eddie said, flipping his wallet closed and returning it to his back pocket.

"Thanks," rang out around the table from all parties.

"My pleasure! Thanks again for taking the time to help out today. Eddie, you can ride with me. I'll bring you back tomorrow to pick up your car."

He had done it again. Cadence didn't want him to get to her, but qualities outside of his arrogance were seeping through and she liked what she saw. Her reasons for avoiding him were waning. As she gathered her belongings and said her goodbyes, she mentally summed up the pros and cons of Blake Barrington. He was successful, gorgeous, funny, caring, charming, and giving, despite being an arrogant playboy and a lawyer.

Blake walked along with Cadence and Alana, waving goodbyes to the others. Once Alana clicked the car alarm, Blake was at Cadence's side, opening her door. She climbed inside. He closed the door and waited for Alana to start the car to roll down the window. Leaning in, he thanked Alana one last time and smiled at Cadence.

"See you Friday?" he asked, curling his full lips into a sexy grin.

Cadence could have sworn she saw a glint in his eye.

"Sure." She knew her response didn't sound assured, but it was the most she could do. Cadence knew she had no intention of going, but didn't want to let him down in front of Alana. She'd let him know sometime during the week that she wouldn't be able to make it. Blake took her hand and kissed it—an unhurried, moist, lingering kiss that offered a stirring indication of how he would handle other parts of her body. A slow burn started in her center. Cadence cleared her throat and shifted in her seat.

"Good night," she said, looking straight forward. She couldn't bring herself to look directly at the hankering in Blake's eyes, afraid she would melt under its heat. Feeling Alana's eyes on her and seeing her wide grin through her peripheral vision, she didn't want to look at her, either. A swollen silence pulsated between them.

"Get home safe," Blake finally said, tapping the side of the car as he stood.

Cadence rolled up her window and before Alana could fix her lips to say something, Cadence pointed a finger at her. "Don't say a word."

"Ha!" Alana obliged, though she couldn't contain her laughter as she put the car in gear and exited the parking lot.

Trying not to be obvious, Cadence watched Blake strut back toward his pickup, closed her eyes and willed the butterflies swarming in her stomach to settle down.

Chapter 9

When Judge Watson banged his gavel, closing out the case in Blake's client's favor, Blake wanted to pump his fist. There was no way that something like that would go over well, especially with this uncompromising judge. Such an unprofessional display would certainly land him in contempt in Watson's courtroom.

Blake's client, Clint Carter, looked stunned, apparently unbelieving of the win. Grabbing the young songwriter's shoulder and reaching out for a handshake, Blake found that he had to shake him a little to get his attention. Instead of offering up his hand, the young man turned his wide shocked eyes toward Blake, wrapped his lanky arms around him and laid his head on his chest.

"Thank you! Thank you! I can't believe this. I couldn't have done this without you!"

"You're welcome, man!" Blake smiled and pulled himself from the viselike embrace and then patted the guy's shoulder.

Blake completely understood Clint's excitement. With the substantial settlement that he was due to receive from the record company that ripped him off, he would be financially set. After sending in his demo recording to be considered for a deal, the young man hadn't heard anything back from the company for months. Then one day, the hopeful artist heard the popular multiplatinum R&B artist J. Reigns singing the words he'd written to the beats he'd created on one of New York's top radio stations. The album went platinum within days.

The jilted songwriter sought Blake out after being referred by another aspiring artist. Always willing to fight for the underdog, Blake took the case without a second thought and fought long and hard against one of the country's largest recording conglomerates to secure this win.

"Go home and celebrate. I'll see you in my office in a few days. I'll have my secretary call you so we can set up a time to get everything closed out. You should have your money in a few short weeks."

"Aw, man. Thank you, man!" Clint cupped Blake's hand in his and shook it vigorously. "I can't believe it, man."

Blake chuckled. "Believe it," he said, stuffing the papers from the table into his briefcase. "You deserve this."

"Woo!" Clint's shout startled Blake, along with a few other lingering folks in the courtroom.

Blake picked up his briefcase and nodded toward the exit. He shared his client's sentiment but didn't want him to get into any trouble. Not only did Clint have a big windfall coming from this settlement, but also the fees due to Barrington and Associates were quite substantial.

Blake exited the court building with a sense of urgency. He needed to make it back to Long Island to meet with the young men of Billy's Promise, the charitable organization where he spent much of his spare time helping young— mainly fatherless—boys blossom into productive men. He had a special treat for the boys tonight. Platinum-selling rapper Iconik was coming for a visit, along with his team from the record company. Blake wanted to expose the boys to all the other jobs in the music industry that were integral to making an artist's career successful. Just the thought of how excited the guys would be when Iconik walked into the center made him smile.

Blake had to make sure everything was all set. This would be more great exposure for the organization. Blake had also invited a few of his own contacts, hoping this didn't turn out to be a media circus.

When Blake arrived at the center, the squeak of sneakers against the wood, laughter and bouncing balls filled the space with youthful energy.

"Yo! What up, Mr. B?," one young man called out. Blake slapped five with several of them as they gathered around.

"I've got something special for y'all tonight," Blake said with a huge grin.

"Was up?" The boys looked at each other with excitement.

"Get everybody together." Blake scanned the group taking a count of how many boys showed up, looking for one in particular. "Where's RaShawn?" he asked when he noticed him missing.

"He's out by the office," another young man said.

"Okay. I need you all to set up about twenty chairs in a semicircle in the middle of the floor. I'll be right back."

"Cool," one young man said, taking the lead as Blake walked off. "Get those chairs and put them right here," he continued giving orders.

Blake greeted Tracy, the after-school site coordinator, as he headed to the back offices. The lights were off. At first he didn't see RaShawn sitting on the floor just beside the door.

"What's up, man? Why are you back here alone?" Blake knew right away that something was wrong, as RaShawn was one of the rambunctious ones in the group.

"I don't feel good."

Concerned, Blake knelt down. "What hurts? Do you have a fever?" Alarm crept over him.

"My stomach."

"Oh. What does it feel like?"

The boy shrugged. "It just hurts."

"Maybe it was something you ate." Blake stood up, feeling the sense of alarm dissipate, assuming the boy probably ate something that didn't agree with him. "What did you have for lunch?"

"I didn't have lunch," the boy said, still holding his head down. He had yet to meet Blake's eyes with his.

"Well, what did you have for breakfast?"

"I ain't had no breakfast, either."

"I didn't…" Blake was about to correct his English but let it pass. He felt bad for the young man. "So you haven't eaten all day?" Blake's expression was twisted in confusion.

"No." RaShawn's head was still down.

"Ray! When was the last time you had something to eat?" Blake demanded.

The boy sighed and silence took up a few beats before he finally answered, "Lunch. Yesterday."

"What!" Blake's hands went to his hips and he sighed. He wanted to ask the boy why but already knew the potential answer. "Okay. Come on and join the group. I don't want you to miss what I have for you guys tonight. I'll get you something to eat."

Blake reached for RaShawn's hand. After a moment, RaShawn placed his hand in Blake's and rose to his feet. Blake pulled out a twenty-dollar bill, folded his business card around it and pressed it into RaShawn's hand. "The next time you get hungry and have no food, you call me! Okay?"

With his head hanging low, RaShawn nodded and stuffed the money and card in his pocket. Blake nudged him in the direction of the other boys and headed to the site coordinator's office.

"Hey, Anita," Blake greeted a young college student who worked at the center after school.

"Hey, Mr. B."

"Can you do me a favor?" Blake continued without awaiting a response, pulling a credit card from his wallet. "Call up the Tastē of Tuscany and order about—" Blake counted mentally "—five pizza pies for the boys. We are also going to have a few guests tonight, so get some drinks and get something for yourself, okay?"

"No problem. And thanks, Mr. B."

Blake walked back out to the main part of the center where the boys were now seated but just as noisy. Clapping his hands, he got their attention. Just as he was about to prep them for their surprise visit, one of the boys said, "Yo, that dude looks like the rapper Iconik!" The rest of the boys and Blake turned around to find Iconik and his crew heading in his direction.

"Your surprise is here!"

The boys jumped from their seats, slapping five with one another, holding their hands over their gaping mouths as Blake walked over to greet their guests.

Iconik and his camp arrived at the same time as the media. Congressman Banks showed up, as well. This high-profile event would be great for his organization. The next two hours were filled with enthusiasm as the boys listened intently to every word their guests had to say. They bombarded Iconik's team with every kind of question, from how much money they made, to what other entertainers they knew personally. Then Iconik took selfies with the kids and a few group photos with Blake and Congressman Banks. Before leaving, he blessed the boys with signed posters, T-shirts and copies of his latest CD.

By the end, not a single strip of edible evidence was left from the pizza and empty juice cups that were sprawled across the floor. Blake looked around at the boys still reeling from their visit and smiled before calling things to order. "All right, guys. We need to get this place cleaned up. Put the chairs back and let's get these pizza boxes and cups in the garbage. We only have a few minutes before we have to shut this down."

The young men quickly obliged, continuing their excited chatter about meeting Iconik in person. Some talked about how they were going to bring their pictures to school to show everyone. Once the space was tidied, some parents arrived and the boys started making their way home. A few of them thanked Blake and others were still too excited to think about it. Blake didn't mind at all, he was just happy to do something that the boys would remember for life.

"I'm proud of you, Blake. Keep up the fine work. One day we'll be running your campaign." Congressman Banks laughed.

"Not sure if I'm cut out for politics, sir. I'll leave that up to you."

"Oh, please! You'd make a fine politician. Just keep your nose clean."

Blake thought about it for a moment and immediately dismissed the idea. He thought about how he'd watched the congressman's life become an open book during his campaign and, as outgoing as he was, he didn't think being so exposed would be very appealing.

"I'll stick to winning cases."

"You do that." Congressman Banks chuckled and then repeated himself, "Yes. You do that." A few seconds of companionable silence settled between them. "Uh, Blake."

"Yes, sir!"

Congressman Banks paused, leaving enough space for Blake to notice a shift in his demeanor. "Have you…" He fell silent once again. "I just want to say I'm proud of you, son."

"Thanks?" Blake's response sounded more like a question. Hadn't Congressman Banks already said he was proud? Blake was proud, too. Seeing the gleam in his boys' eyes felt as good as winning a case.

"This was a great thing you did here. Let's touch base soon."

"Sure," Blake replied.

The next instant, Banks was gone. His behavior struck Blake as odd. Blake wondered if the congressman had left something unsaid, but he dismissed his suspicions. If something was wrong, Banks would reveal it to him soon enough. Banks had gotten into the habit of sending clients Blake's way, in addition to having him handle many of his own legal transactions. He knew that Blake wasn't interested in being a politician but maintained that it was always beneficial to make the right connections.

Outside the center, as Anita locked up, Blake found himself wondering what Cadence would have thought about today's visit. Blake recalled his father's words, "It's nice to have great experiences and nice things, but it's even better when you have someone to share them with." He pictured Cadence being the one he could share his victories and spoils with and found himself wondering how she would respond.

With her cool demeanor, he imagined her pretty smile and approving nod. Blake shook his head as if to rid himself of those thoughts and then released a wholehearted laugh. He found it extremely amusing that he daydreamed about a woman. He didn't know what it was about Cadence Payne that had him so smitten, but he vowed he'd find out, looking forward to enjoying the discovery process as much as possible.

Then again, he knew exactly what it was that reeled him in. Besides that fact that she was extremely attractive in a way that exuded simple elegance, she held a quiet confidence that was intriguing. Unlike many of the over-the-top women that grappled for his attention, Cadence didn't seem to care if he was interested in her or not. She didn't need gobs of makeup blanketing her face, thirty inches of weave cascading down her back or the boastful labels of high-end brand names clinging to her curves. She was a woman of substance—a rarity who seemed to know her worth.

Cadence was also a challenge. Not a challenge he wanted to overcome just to prove that he could. Cadence was worth fighting for and worth all the effort that came with the fight even if the win was a pyrrhic victory.

With renewed focus, Blake was ready for their impending date. He couldn't wait to spend time with her.

Chapter 10

The week had been long and challenging. Cleaning up Richard McLennan's mess had dominated the top of Cadence's task list. During her visit to his office the previous week, the truth about what really happened was revealed, which was even more absurd than Richard's original account. Fortunately, they were able to talk him out of trying to press assault charges against his secretary for blackening his eye after he blatantly squeezed her behind as he wagged his tongue. It was clear that Richard was the common denominator to all of their company's harassment issues.

The current week had been filled with conference calls and meetings between Cadence's firm and Victoria's lawyers to reach a new settlement offer. In an effort to save the face of the company, the board urged Richard to take a leave and get himself together. Richard's cousin, the company's vice president, had been put in place to run the company in his absence. Victoria—she resigned and received a sizable severance agreement.

Things had finally settled down. At least she thought so until her secretary came bursting through her office door looking as though she was trying to escape a herd of bulls. Taking a deep breath, Amy heaved out a sigh before she spoke. At first her words came out so fast that Cadence couldn't understand what she had said.

Gasping for another breath and holding it for a moment, Amy tried to speak again. "They gave Kerry the position of senior counsel," she huffed. Amy looked behind her and then closed the door.

"What?" Cadence was on her feet immediately.

Still hanging on to the knob, Amy locked the door and slumped into the chair in front of Cadence's desk. "They gave her the position, Cadence. She's been promoted to senior counsel."

Cadence's legs wobbled beneath her. She grabbed the sides of her chair and guided her body into it. "They did?" she said ever so slightly.

"The suits made the decision today," she said, referring to the firm's executive team.

Cadence's shoulders slumped. She didn't bother asking Amy how she knew. Amy was close friends with one of the senior partner's secretaries and always got the information before it hit the mainstream. Distress burned inside of her. She wanted that position so bad and worked so hard to get it. As supportive as she was, she couldn't bring herself to be happy for Kerry. She felt as if the position had been swiped from under her. What happened? Couldn't they see that Kerry was mischievous? Had Kerry done something to sabotage her chances? Had she mentioned the fact that she'd referred to Richard McLennan as a sleazebag? Did this have anything to do with Kerry's father, who was a broadcasting icon? Maybe he pulled some strings for her.

These questions and more paraded through Cadence's mind like a stampede. She looked up into Amy's eyes and saw a reflection of how she felt. Amy was clearly disappointed, too.

"How did you find out?" Cadence asked anyway, her face still holding her weary expression.

"Adam's secretary, Christine, told me. They called Kerry upstairs a few moments ago to tell her. Christine said not to tell anyone, but I couldn't keep this from you. You deserved to know. That position should have been yours."

Cadence closed her mouth, which she realized had been gaping. Swallowing hard, she pushed down the lump in her throat. "Thank you for giving me the heads-up, Amy."

"They're about to call a meeting to announce it to everyone in the office. I didn't want you to be blindsided."

Cadence's eyes stung. She didn't want to cry in front of Amy. She sat more rigidly, trying to fight her emotions. Lifting her chin, she said, "Hey. We can't win them all," and was thankful that her voice didn't quiver.

Amy's shoulders slumped and she pressed her lips together in a sympathetic smile, obviously not buying Cadence's act. Standing, Amy took one more deep breath and, with her head down, she quietly exited Cadence's office.

The second the door shut, the tears fell. Cadence couldn't help it. She stood, slowly walked to the window and folded her arms across her torso as she looked down at the traffic on Sixth Avenue. Kerry was a shark, and she played the office-politics game well, only baring her teeth to those who couldn't hinder her climb. She couldn't be mad at her for winning. Cadence reasoned that it just wasn't her time. She was a dedicated attorney who worked hard for her clients. Cadence's arms dropped to her sides. Her phone rang.

Picking up the office phone, she cleared her throat before answering. "Cadence Payne speaking." She hoped the caller couldn't detect the distress in her voice.

"Cadence! Can you come to my office, please?"

"Sure, Mr. Benjamin," she obliged, recognizing his voice. "I'll be right there." She tried her best to sound normal.

Cadence pulled out her purse, retrieved a small mirror and checked her face. Her eyes were a little red, so she put in a few drops that she normally used for her contacts. Wiping the excess fluid away, she reexamined her image and added a layer of gloss on her lips to freshen her face as much as possible. She couldn't go into Adam's office looking like a sore loser.

Taking a deep breath, she closed her eyes and exhaled. Before opening the door, she straightened her back and pasted a smile on her face. Her eyes connected with Amy's as she passed her desk. Amy smiled and held her thumbs up, turning Cadence's painted smile into a genuine one.

Standing taller, Cadence stepped off the elevator and was greeted by the stoic portraits of former partners. The level that housed the executive offices maintained a sense of luxury that was absent on the lower level. Cadence's floor resembled a maze of gray fabric cubicles, with smaller offices along the perimeter—one of which belonged to her. As her heels clicked against the marble floors, she ran her fingers across the solid mahogany wainscoting. The walk to Adam's office seemed longer than usual.

Adam's door was open, but Cadence lifted her hand to knock anyway. Just before she made contact, Adam summoned her in.

"Hello, Ms. Payne," he said, looking up from the documents he was scanning.

"Mr. Benjamin." Cadence nodded. His formal address gave her pause.

"Please!" He stood. "Have a seat," he said, gesturing toward the chair.

Cadence sat slow and easy, watching Adam as he rounded his mahogany desk to close the door and lock it. Cadence folded and unfolded her hands and nervous energy surged through her. She continued watching as Adam made his way back to his chair.

"Ms. Payne." She swallowed. "Cadence." He readdressed her more informally. Adam looked at her, cleared his throat and sat back for a beat before speaking. "I want you to know that you are a valued member of this team."

Cadence checked her emotions, already knowing where this was going. Being told how much of a "valued team member" you were was always a prelude to bad news. She braced herself and fiddled with her hands.

"We had a very hard decision to make in choosing the right candidate to advance to the position of senior counsel. This time, Kerry Cooper was selected. This is in no way a reflection on your performance." Adam sat back.

Cadence took her time responding, unsure of how steady her voice would be when she did speak. "I understand. I must congratulate Kerry when I see her," she managed to say. Usually, she had no problem being the consummate professional, but this time, keeping her composure proved to be difficult. The sting of disappointment pricked at her professional exterior.

Adam rose from his seat. He sat on the corner of the desk, closer to Cadence.

"If this decision was mine alone to make..." Adam shrugged his shoulders, his body language finishing his statement.

Cadence was beginning to see the situation more clearly. Adam had her back, but the other decision makers hadn't been rooting for her.

Several beats lagged by before Adam started again.

"It's just a matter of time…" He paused. "I recommend—"
There was a tap on the office door. Both Cadence and
Adam stared at the door for a second before Adam called
out, "One moment." He flashed Cadence a quick glance
that seemed to ask if she caught his drift.

She did.

The tap came again, this time a little louder. Adam
opened the door to find his secretary on the other side.

Cadence stood at once, feeling as if they'd been caught
doing something. "Thank you, Mr. Benjamin," she said
and smiled at Christine as she exited between them.

Cadence couldn't get back to her office quick enough.
She pressed the call button for the elevator repeatedly as if
the more she pressed it the faster it would come. She was
intelligent and could read between the lines. She needed
to work a little harder at being noticed. She had to admit
that was one thing that Kerry did well.

The elevator came and Cadence entered so deep in
thought that she was oblivious to the other riders. She
stepped out on her floor and headed straight for her office,
closing the door behind her. She plopped down in her chair
and considered for the first time that Adam may have had
more to say. When his secretary opened that door, she saw
that as an opportunity to escape. She needed to get out of
there before she fell apart.

Adam had planted seeds of new possibilities with what
he'd left unsaid. Cadence hadn't thought about leaving the
firm before and wondered if he may have suggested that.
Perhaps even open up her own practice. That was something else to consider.

Cadence's cell phone rang and Blake's number lit the
display. Her week was so hectic she had forgotten about
calling him to cancel their date. She waited for a moment,
thinking of an excuse. After all that went on today, she
didn't think she'd make good company anyway.

"Hello," she finally answered just before the call went to voice mail.

"Good afternoon, Ms. Payne." Blake's deep sultry voice filled the line.

As much as she hated to admit it, the mere sound of his voice caused the layers of her skin to tingle.

"Hey, Blake." She tried to sound unaffected.

"Looking forward to tonight? I just wanted to let you know to wear something casual and comfortable that you wouldn't mind getting a little dirty. I'll be there at seven thirty."

"Uh… Blake."

"Nope!"

Cadence's brows creased. "Huh? What do you mean, nope?"

"You can't cancel on me. I knew you'd try."

Cadence rolled her eyes. She felt bad, but she was in no mood to hang out with anyone, let alone tall, handsome, gorgeous Blake. "I'm sorry, Blake, but I'm having a really bad day."

"Good. Then what I have planned will be a perfect way to end a horrible day on a great note. See you at seven thirty."

Blake hung up before she could protest. Cadence slid her cell across her desk and dropped her head, resting it on the back of her chair. Going out with Blake would probably be better than sitting at home alone mulling over the fact that she didn't get the promotion. Moreover, it didn't look as if Blake was willing to accept no for an answer.

Blake told her to wear something casual and comfortable that she wouldn't mind getting dirty. What kind of dirty was he talking about?

Chapter 11

Blake couldn't believe that he was actually nervous. In fact, the feeling felt foreign to him. He laughed at how fidgety he'd become while getting dressed. It took much longer than usual to button up his cotton shirt. Checking his reflection several times, he rolled up his sleeves, then rolled them down before just changing into a short-sleeved shirt. He had even forgotten to put on a belt until the very last minute.

The consummate ladies' man, going out on a date never made him sweat. Tonight's date wasn't with just any woman. This was Cadence Payne, daughter of a senator and the one woman he couldn't manage to get off his mind. He'd made every effort to make careful plans—even called in a few favors. This night should leave a lasting impression, and he hoped that his penchant to test his boundaries wouldn't send her running. Blake simply wanted to do something different. They could go to dinner and a movie once he was able to secure his hooks in her heart.

Blake knew what he wanted—basically, all of her. However, he knew he had to take his time with Cadence. She had to be nudged gently until she came to the realization that she wanted him, too. Attraction wasn't the issue. Blake always knew when women were attracted to him. Cadence was trying to fight it. He wasn't sure why, but somehow he was going to get her to take the gloves off.

After jumping into his truck, Blake punched in the address that Cadence had texted to him earlier. His GPS indicated that she lived only fifteen minutes away. The second he turned the key in the ignition, firing up the large SUV with a roar, another sliver of nervousness surged through him. Cadence hadn't sounded that enthusiastic about going out when he'd called her earlier. She did respond to his text asking for the address, so he was confident that she wasn't going to cancel the date.

With time to spare, Blake pulled up in front of her townhome. He sat for a moment, not wanting to appear too eager. Using the spare minutes he had, he made calls to ensure his plans for the evening would go over smoothly. Everything was set. Blake pushed the car door open with renewed confidence. It was time to get his girl.

Blake pressed the bell and Cadence pulled the door open, filling the entrance with her splendor and a thousand-volt smile.

"Hello." Her voice felt like a soft caress.

"Hey, yourself." Blake couldn't help licking his lips.

Cadence nodded and stepped back to let him in the house. "Come have a seat. I'll be ready in a moment."

Taking in the glorious way her thighs and behind filled in her jeans and the sway of her hips made Blake suck in his bottom lip and take a deep breath. When it came to Cadence, it wasn't just about her physical magnificence; it was her coolness, her confident gait and her simple beauty. She wore her signature ponytail, which cascaded halfway down her back. She wasn't skinny by any stretch of the imagination, nor was she a hefty girl. As far as Blake was concerned, she was just right. He thought it shameful how women fought against their voluptuousness to meet the media's so-called standard. Cadence was perfect. He hoped she knew it, and if she didn't, he'd help her realize it.

Blake sat on the sofa, sizing up the living room. It was a direct reflection of her personality—a cool, comfortable space, nicely designed but not overdone. As Blake looked around, he caught a glimpse of an interesting piece of black-and-white art. He walked to the hallway and stopped, looking for Cadence. He could hear her moving around upstairs. Continuing, he moved to the painting, admiring the abstract masterpiece.

"Like it?" Cadence's smooth voice collapsed his concentration.

Blake turned toward her, washing his gaze over her from top to bottom. "As a matter of fact, I do."

"The charcoal, silly!" Cadence cut her eyes and shook her head.

"That, too," he said, still admiring the work of art that was Cadence.

She stood beside him and he took in the sweet floral scent of her. Blake knew right then that self-control could be an issue for him.

"It's beautiful," he said. "I find abstract work very interesting. Who is it by?"

"Me," Cadence said and turned toward him. She held up the two pairs of shoes she had in her hand. "Which ones?"

"Wear the ones that are most comfortable. Now, back to the painting. You really did this?" he asked, surprised. He hadn't pegged her for the artist type. This made her even more intriguing. "What was your inspiration?"

"I was missing my mother one day and I drew her face.

The abstract part came after but fit what I was feeling at the time. Then I fell in love with it, so I hung it there."

Blake glanced down the hallway, which looked like a charcoal exhibit at a gallery. "You did all of these?"

"Yes," she said and then quickly changed the subject. "I'm ready."

Blake let it go. She'd already had a bad day and he didn't want to drum up sad memories that would put her in a mournful mood. He quickly checked out the other images. Blake was so taken by her collection that he hadn't noticed that she'd finally slipped on her shoes, grabbed her purse and was standing at the door.

"So, where are we going?" she asked, twisting her keys in her hands.

"To try something new."

Cadence smiled and Blake liked what he saw. As they headed out, he decided that he wanted to become the one who was always responsible for putting a smile on her face.

Blake helped her into the SUV and jogged around to the driver's side. He tapped the screen on the dashboard and the sounds of Joe's latest release serenaded them. "What would you like to listen to?"

"This is fine. I love Joe," Cadence said and turned her head toward the passenger window.

Blake started the engine but didn't move. Her brief answers and more than cool demeanor let him know that she hadn't shaken off the horrible day she said she'd had. He turned to Cadence and stared at her until she felt his gaze.

Cadence scrunched her brows. "What?" she quizzed.

"I need you to let go of your day."

Cadence dropped her shoulders. "I'm sorry. I am trying. I guess it still shows."

"Allow me." Blake put his hands on her shoulders.

Cadence turned to face the passenger window, letting Blake knead away the tension knotted in her shoulders.

Cadence closed her eyes and let his powerful hands work on her. "That feels good." She moaned and arched her back when Blake hit a tight spot. "Oops." She chuckled. "Sorry."

"No apology necessary." Her moan was like music to Blake's ears.

Cadence rolled her neck as Blake continued to massage her shoulders.

"You've got talented hands," she said and then paused abruptly, turning toward Blake.

He smiled, knowing that she was looking for him to take her statement and turn it into a seductive innuendo.

"As tempting as that was, I'm going to let it ride."

They both chuckled. Blake finished his massage and Cadence thanked him.

"Now, before we go, I need you to offload the rest of that tension from today. Tell me what happened."

"Blake…"

Blake held up his hand in protest. "I've got great plans for us…" He paused to let his comment hang for a while before adding, "Tonight. I don't want anything hindering us from having a great time. So do us both a favor and unload. Get it out so you don't have to deal with it anymore."

Cadence huffed and proceeded to give Blake a play-by-play about how horrible her day was and even admitted that she felt bad for not being happy for Kerry.

"It's simple," Blake said.

"What's simple?"

"It's time to move on. If they don't want to recognize your brilliance, go somewhere that will. Better yet, start your own firm." Blake looked over at the surprised look on Cadence's face. "What? You are brilliant, aren't you?"

"Well…"

"Yes!" Blake finished the sentence for her.

"I have thought about it, but it's not easy." Cadence sighed and let her head fall against the headrest as if she had the weight of the world resting on her.

"Cadence." Blake turned to her. "You know your worth, don't you?"

"Of course!" Cadence almost looked offended.

"Are you good at what you do?"

"Damn good!"

Blake smiled at her show of confidence. "That's what I'm talking about. Then nothing can stop you from being successful. Not even those blind decision makers at your firm. If you think you're ready, just do it or at least start the process."

Cadence's eyes held a faraway look, as if she was calculating what Blake had just said. He let the conversation marinate as he put the SUV in gear.

"Oh! I want to show you something," Blake said, reaching into the backseat. He pulled out a newspaper and placed it on Cadence's lap. "Turn to page ten."

Cadence did as he said. "Wow." She smiled at the photo of him with a group of boys, famed rapper Iconik and Congressman Banks. "When did you take this?"

"Last week. I brought Iconik to the center to talk to the boys that I mentor about jobs in the industry."

"That's great! Where's the center?"

"It's in Hempstead. The organization I mentor with uses it for their after-school program."

"Which organization?"

"It's called Billy's Promise. It was started by Congressman Banks. It's his way of offering fatherless boys a chance to connect with positive role models. He grew up without a father."

Cadence raised her brows. "Impressive," she said.

"Yeah. I love working with those kids. They're a little crazy but still cool." He took in the music of Cadence's laughter. "All right, enough of that!" Blake took the newspaper and tossed it into the backseat. "Let's go enjoy the night."

Cadence smiled again and Blake smiled on the inside.

Chapter 12

As reluctant as Cadence was about going out with Blake, she had to admit that she was enjoying every minute of it. From the second she opened the door and found his handsome face staring back at her, smiling with a perfect set of bright white teeth, she was glad she had agreed to go.

On their ride to Manhattan, Cadence stole glances at him, admiring his striking profile. She watched as his strong masculine hands fingered the controls on the dashboard and even found herself thinking about how those same strong hands had worked away the tension in her shoulders moments before. The memory made her have to control the shudder that threatened to roll through her body.

Blake announced that they were approaching their first stop but still hadn't given her any clues about the night's plans. All she knew was that they might get dirty. Cadence smirked when she thought about it. Blake pulled the SUV into a parking garage and they strolled through the streets of Lower Manhattan. They arrived at the entrance of a swanky-looking restaurant, but Cadence stopped short when she saw the name, Sex on the Palate.

Rearing her head back, she cast him a sideways glare. "Uh… Blake? What is this?" She waited for his response before reacting. He couldn't have brought her to some raunchy strip club on the first date. The place didn't look questionable. She was confused.

Blake took her by the hand. "Just trust me."

Cadence narrowed her eyes at him as she followed him in. Once inside, an attractive man wearing a chef's coat with a five-o'clock shadow and blond wisps of hair hanging over his eyes greeted Blake.

Blake turned to Cadence. "I'd like you to meet my lady friend, the lovely Cadence." Blake presented her with pride. Cadence smiled and shook the chef's hand, who immediately excused himself after a friendly greeting.

Cadence looked around and thought about how interesting this placed looked for a food establishment.

"It's a cooking school," Blake finally said.

"Oh! We're here for a lesson?"

"That and more." Blake winked.

Cadence narrowed her eyes but quickly shifted her scolding glare when the chef returned with aprons for the two of them. Cadence felt much more comfortable. She looked over at Blake, who wore a mischievous smile, and playfully punched him in the arm before putting on her apron.

"You shouldn't have such a dirty mind," he teased. "This place is one of the finest in the world for aphrodisiac cooking. It's more than just a cooking class. It's an experience," Blake said, raising his brows two quick times before following the chef to their cooking area.

Cadence shook her head. As the evening progressed, she allowed herself to be wrapped up into the sensual vibe created by the wine and soft music flowing from the hidden speakers. The chef guided them through the preparation of their meal, educating them on the effects and purpose of every ingredient. Not only was this turning out to be fine cooking, but it was also a titillating experience for the senses. Everything excited her, from the feel of the food, to the fragrance of the spices, and the savory flavors of each dish.

Their three-course meal consisted of an appetizer with roasted fennel. The chef advised that it was an estrogen enhancer. Their entrée boasted chicken with chocolate butter and, for dessert, a delectable brioche bread pudding topped with strawberries and a drizzle of chocolate sauce. The slight hint of spice seemed to warm Cadence on the inside.

The cacophony of fragrant aromas and intense spices teased her senses. Every morsel was delicious and Cadence had pretty much let all of her defenses down by time dessert was served. By then, they were feeding each other.

When they left, Cadence could feel the effects of all the foods she'd indulged in. Blood seemed to rush to certain areas, heightening her sensitivities. A simple brush of Blake's hand ignited small fires along her skin. Conversation flowed more easily as her inhibitions waned—her euphoria induced by the meal and wine. She found herself giggling at every silly thing Blake said. She had no idea that eating could be so intoxicating.

"We have one more stop to make."

"Where to?" Cadence didn't mind the time. She was enjoying herself and didn't want the night to end anyway.

"You'll see!"

Cadence had to focus on keeping her loins in check. Blake wasn't helping at all. All he had to do was flash one of those sexy smiles, show off those cavernous crevices on his cheeks that most called dimples or walk in that manly way he always did and warmth would spread through her.

Cadence was determined to stick the night out, but she'd have to avoid going out on future dates with Blake. He was a hazard to her willfulness, chipping away at it with every push of the envelope. Their first date wasn't even halfway over and he had her teetering dangerously on the edge.

A few blocks away they entered what looked like a home-decorating shop. Beautiful urns and vases lined the shelves and floors. A cheerful chime let the staff know that new customers had arrived. Cadence admired the pottery while a slight woman with a huge smile came from the back in a smock and merrily addressed Blake by name. They hugged and Cadence felt a slight twinge of jealousy. She turned away, pretending to be interested in the vases and watching their interaction from her peripheral vision.

"Beth. This is my lovely lady friend, Cadence."

Cadence waltzed over with a confident smile. Nodding her head, she held her hand out to Beth. "It's nice to meet you."

Beth pushed her hand aside. "Oh, girl. I'm a hugger!" She wrapped her arms around Cadence, giving her no choice but to oblige.

The super friendly greeting washed away Cadence's jealous prickling.

"I'm all ready for you. Just follow me," Beth said, waving her hand as she turned and walked through a curtain leading to a pottery studio. "Cadence, you can sit here, and Blake—" Beth pointed to a pottery wheel next to Cadence "—you can sit right there. Give me a moment and I'll give you a quick tutorial. You can choose your pottery and the vase or bowl you'd like to make and I'll get you all set up."

Cadence looked over at Blake and gave him an appreciative smile. This date had been the best she could remember. Blake had gone out of his way to make this night unique. If she never saw him again, she'd always remember tonight.

Beth got them situated and started them off with the pottery wheels. Cadence followed her instructions to the letter, pressing her clay into the wheel and then dipping her hands into the bucket of water next to her. Cradling the clay, Cadence began molding it into a cone. The feel of the clay between her hands as she stroked it up and down brought naughty thoughts to her mind. This date had her on sensory overload. She was going to need a cold shower when she got home.

Chimes rang, indicating that someone had entered the shop. Beth promised them she'd be right back, leaving instructions for them to continue throwing the clay just as she taught them. She also reminded them to keep their hands wet so the mold wouldn't dry out. When she left, Blake stared at Cadence. Once again, her body warmed under the scrutiny of his gaze.

Cadence happened to look down at the warped clay that Blake was molding and burst out laughing. Hers was perfect. His, on the other hand, looked like a three-year-old had been at the wheel.

"Hey! Don't laugh at me," Blake said, laughing himself.

"You have to do it like this," Cadence said, sliding her hands up and down the clay the way Beth had showed her. Blake stretched his eyes at the motion of her hands, and when Cadence looked down, she realized how suggestive her movements were. Laughing hysterically, Cadence absentmindedly covered her mouth to stifle her laugh and ended up getting clay on her face. Imagining how ridiculous she must have looked, she laughed even harder. Blake joined in and Cadence reached over and wiped some of the clay across his nose.

"Now stop laughing at me!"

"Are we being naughty?" Beth appeared with her hands on her hips and her lips pursed before laughing herself. "I see we are getting acquainted with the clay."

Everyone laughed at that.

"Okay. Let's move on so you can have a great piece of pottery to take home with you."

Cadence got serious. She was looking forward to making something beautiful to commemorate this night. Beth worked with her to mold and bake a lovely vase that she eventually painted yellow, her favorite color. She was proud of her accomplishment.

Blake hadn't improved. At one point, he got frustrated and squeezed his clay a little too hard, sending chucks of it around the room. Most of it landed on him and a little on Cadence and Beth. Cadence was doubled over laughing as he tried to peel the chunks off his shirt and add them back to the clay still spinning on the wheel. The shape he created was unidentifiable, but he painted it anyway.

After letting them dry for a while, Beth bagged their creations up and Blake thanked her for extending herself beyond her normal studio hours. With dried clay clinging to their shirts and their masterpieces in hand, they snaked their way through the tons of people still walking the city streets after dark. Blake reached for Cadence's hand. She didn't pull back. Hand in hand, they took their time getting to the parking garage.

Drained from the intensity of the evening's activities, Cadence fell asleep on the ride back home. When she finally opened her eyes, they were sitting in front of her house.

"I didn't mean to fall asleep on you," she said, stretching and yawning.

"No problem. You were sleeping so good, I didn't want to wake you. So I just sat here and watched you."

Cadence blushed, but to Blake she said, "That's creepy,"

and laughed. "Well," she started and paused. "I guess this is it." As tired as she was, she still didn't want this night to end. She wanted to invite him in but decided against it. He couldn't think she was easy prey. She also reminded herself that she didn't have the mental or emotional capacity to add dating to her plate. This would have to be it for them.

"Well," Blake said, falling silent as she had just a moment before.

"Thank you for a wonderful night." she said, taking note of the disappointment in his eyes.

Blake smiled. "You are most certainly welcome."

"Good night," she said, but hadn't gotten out of the car. Wanting to take her time, she let another beat pass before resting her hand on the car door handle. "I guess I should go now."

Blake raised his brows but didn't utter a word. Reluctantly, Cadence pushed the door open and got out.

"Let me walk you to your door." Blake exited, rounded the car, took the bag she was holding with her pottery and walked her to her door.

Even though they took measured steps, they reached the door too fast. Turning to face each other, Cadence thanked him one last time and reached for her package. Blake's eyes burned with desire, stirring her sensibilities once again. Instead of handing Cadence the vase, he gently placed it down on the porch. When he stood, he captured her with his heated gaze once again. Then without warning, he cupped her face in his hands, pulled her to him and covered her mouth with his. Cadence melted under his touch. Her knees grew weak. Longing ignited in her belly like fireworks.

The intensity of their kiss increased quickly and they devoured each other's lips. Pulling away only for the sake of breathing, Blake held her face in his hands, leaning his forehead against hers. Together they panted, gasping for air.

Without another word, Blake bent over, picked up her vase and waited for her to open her door. She walked in slowly. When she had made it inside, he handed her the vase, winked, and pulled the door closed. Cadence knew how long it took him to get to the car, how long he sat inside without moving and exactly what time he finally pulled off—all because she was watching from her window.

No, she couldn't continue this…this thing with Blake. He was too much. He'd have her living on the edge, breaking her own rules. She wouldn't be able to concentrate.

She touched her lips, still feeling his against hers. No. She couldn't put herself in a position to get hurt again. Cadence put her vase down, pulled out her cell phone and deleted his contact information.

Chapter 13

Cadence reached her hand toward the nightstand and fumbled for her cell phone. Dragging it to her ear, she hadn't even bothered to look to see who was calling.

"Hello," she croaked, cleared her throat and repeated it again. "Hello."

"Still in bed, huh? How's my baby girl?"

"Hey, Dad," Cadence sat up, pushing aside the damp sheets that clung to her legs. She hadn't turned on the air-conditioning last night before falling asleep, and with the amount of heat her memory foam mattress held, she felt as if she'd slept in a sauna. "How's it going?" She swung her legs over the side of the bed and stretched.

"Well, you know," he said, referring to his duties as senator. "More of this and more of that. You wouldn't believe the amount of crap your president has to deal with in these meetings." Her father's exaggerated exhale filled the line with his unspoken frustrations. "I didn't call to talk about work. I just wanted to check in on you. How's it going?"

"Work was crazy this week, but I don't want to talk about that now. I'll let you in on the details when you get back." Cadence looked at the clock, noticing it was just past ten in the morning. She'd slept much later than normal and had even missed her Saturday-morning meet up with her running group. "When do you get back?"

"I'll be home Wednesday."

"Okay." Her mouth spread into a yawn before she knew it. "Oh goodness! Excuse me, Dad!"

Senator Payne chuckled. "No problem, sweetie. I'm getting off this phone anyway. Go on and get your rest. Don't make any plans for Wednesday evening. I plan on taking you to dinner."

"Looking forward to it," she said, suppressing another yawn.

Cadence ended the call, replaced the phone on the nightstand and fell back on the bed. She hadn't slept this late in a while. A smile spread across her face when she remembered why. Her date with Blake had been amazing.

As if on cue, her cell phone rang again. This time it was Alana.

"Tell me all about it," Alana said, nearly cutting off Cadence's greeting.

"Jeez! Can I finish saying hello?"

"Yeah. Hi! Whatever! Now tell me. How did it go?"

The blush warmed Cadence's cheek. She would never admit it, but just thinking about the night she shared with Blake perked her up. She proceeded to give her best friend a play-by-play, being careful not to leave out any important details. Alana wouldn't have had it any other way.

"Oh! That sounds so sexy! That Blake! I tell you!" Alana hooted. "I just love the fact that he didn't take you on a regular ole dinner-and-a-movie kind of date. Not that there's anything wrong with that. Girl, he's worth keeping. He gets ten points for originality."

Cadence laughed.

"And wait. What was the name of that place again? Sexy Table?"

Cadence could hear Alana rummaging around, possibly looking for a pen to write down the name of the restaurant.

"Sex on the Palate."

"I need to make a note of that. I've never heard of aphrodisiac cooking before. I've got to check this place out when I find a new man." Alana laughed. "So, when are you going out again?"

"I don't know." Knowing that wasn't enough of an answer for Alana, she said it anyway, hoping to buy some time.

"You haven't decided."

"Not exactly."

"Wait a minute!" Alana said. Cadence knew that she was reading into her resistance. "Don't tell me you're trying to give Blake the brush-off."

"Not exactly," Cadence repeated.

"This is me you're talking to. What's the problem, Cay? I don't understand."

"It's just that…the timing isn't quite right."

"Are you kidding me? It's summer. Love is in the air. Give me one good reason why you shouldn't continue seeing him."

"Work…"

"Bull crap!" Alana interjected.

"Alana!"

"Cadence! Work is not an excuse to avoid dating a fine, brilliant, creative man like Blake. Why are you afraid?"

Cadence was silent, afraid to voice her fears. They were real enough as it was. Besides, she knew Alana would shoot them down as if they didn't matter. They did matter—to her.

Alana released a heavy sigh. "Cay. You have to let go of

the past and get back in the game. You're depriving yourself of potential happiness. Work will always be there, and most important, he's not Kenny!"

Maybe it was time to move on. Kenny certainly had. She wasn't shocked to see him on that new reality show with his new wife. He was finally in the spotlight. Cadence sincerely hoped he was happy. Cadence flopped back on the bed and crossed her feet on the headboard.

"Look at how much fun you had last night. You really enjoyed yourself. I could hear it in your voice. You can't let fear of getting hurt keep you from living," Alana pleaded.

Cadence wanted to get off the phone. She didn't feel like being preached to right now. Didn't Alana think that she knew these things? Knowing them and acting on them were two different things. Cadence had gotten used to her safe, solemn existence and she was fine with it.

"What's up for today?" Alana asked.

Cadence was thankful that her friend knew when to change the subject. "Nothing much other than to try to figure out what I'm going to do about my job."

"Find another firm and leave!"

Cadence rolled her eyes. "You're the second person who told me to leave. It's not that easy."

"Yes it is. You can even just start your own practice," Alana encouraged.

Cadence felt as if this was déjà vu. "Blake said the same thing."

"So what's stopping you? There are dozens of firms out there. Girl!" Alana sucked her teeth. "Step out on faith. You can call your firm Payne and Associates."

Despite her resistance, Cadence did like the sound of that.

"Just because those crabs don't want you to be successful, that doesn't mean you won't become successful. Start your firm and whup their butts in court. They'll wish they had never overlooked you," Alana said.

That put a smile on Cadence's face. "That's true. I'll start looking into it. I'll give myself a while to get things in motion."

"That's my girl! All you—"

"Oh!" Cadence interrupted, "Hold on, I'm getting another call." Cadence looked at her phone but didn't recognize the number. She had already spoken to her father, so she wondered who else would be calling her on a Saturday morning. "One sec, Alana. Let me see who this is." Cadence swiped the other call in. "Hello," she answered in her professional tone.

"Hey, beautiful." A tiny shudder sparked in her gut and radiated outward at the sound of Blake's voice.

"Hey." She remembered that she had deleted him from her contacts. "What's up?"

"I hope I didn't scare you off after last night. I just wanted to make sure our first night together was memorable."

"Oh." Cadence sucked her teeth and waved her hand dismissively as she lied through those same teeth. "Not at all." The truth was, he did scare her—in many ways. Her defenses were waning due to him, and it wasn't just because of the aphrodisiacs they'd feasted on. Then she remembered the kiss. Cadence didn't think she could let herself become vulnerable to a man as risqué as Blake. Surely she'd end up with a broken heart.

"Got plans today?"

"No." Cadence scrunched her face and tightened her fist, scolding herself for answering so fast. No woman ever wanted to seem as if they were always readily available. "Actually, I planned to stay at home today and take care of a few things and get some much-needed rest. I've been working a lot of long hours lately."

"How about you relax tomorrow?"

Cadence lifted a single brow. "You can be bossy sometimes, you know."

Blake laughed and Cadence practically melted right there in her bed. "It's not a matter of being bossy. When I know what I want, I go after it."

If the sound of his laughter didn't make her entire being go limp, that last comment almost did. He wanted her and he was making no bones about it. "Okay," she said, stretching out the word. The phone beeped, indicating that she was getting another call. She remembered that she had Alana on the other line and gasped. "Oh no! Hold on, Blake, please." Swiping in the other call, Cadence said, "Alana, I'm so sorry."

"Did you forget about me? That better be that fine-ass Blake on the other end. That's the only acceptable excuse for leaving me hanging."

Cadence chuckled and then blushed again. "As a matter of fact, it is. He was asking what I was doing today."

"And…?"

"I've got a lot to do around here, so—"

"Didn't you say you had fun last night?" Alana interrupted her again.

"Yes, but—"

"But nothing! Forget about sitting around the house. Go out and have some more fun. If it works out, then that's great. If it doesn't, then move on. In the meantime, ride that sucker until the wheels blow out like cheap tires on a road trip! Go on and talk to that man." Alana chuckled. "Call me later."

Alana hung right up. Cadence swiped the screen on her cell phone to return to Blake's call.

"Sorry about that," she said and pushed herself up from the bed. She paced the floor.

"No problem. Now, back to us. Are you going to hang out with me today?"

Cadence groaned. Should she go or not? She thought about what Alana had just said. *If it works out, then that's great. If it doesn't, then move on. In the meantime, ride that sucker...* She chuckled at Alana's funny twist to the old cliché. *At least you'll have fun in the process.*

"Well?" Blake interrupted her personal debating session.

"What the hell! There's always tomorrow." Cadence pushed her doubts aside. Being with Blake felt good. It heightened her senses. Besides, she wasn't looking to fall in love with the guy. "What time should I expect you?"

"I'll be there by one," Blake said.

Cadence looked at the time on her phone. It was almost noon. "That doesn't give me much time!" She panicked.

"You don't need much time."

That made her smile. "How should I dress?"

"Comfortably."

"Okay. See you at one!" she said, containing her excitement.

"Can't wait." His sexy voice filled the line.

Cadence blushed and ended the call without saying goodbye. She ran into the bathroom for a quick shower, and returned to her closet to assess her wardrobe as she brushed her teeth. Pulling out a couple of maxi dresses, she laid them on her bed and put her free hand on her hip while she decided on what to wear. Finally, she selected a green multicolored strapless number that cinched at the waist and flowed gracefully to the heels of her feet. It was as beautiful as it was comfortable. Matching it with yellow flats, her favorite diamond stud earrings and a thin chain with a studded cross, she managed a casual feel.

Time got away from her and before she knew it, Blake was knocking at her door. She still hadn't eaten breakfast, so she grabbed her purse and a banana from the fruit bowl she kept on her kitchen table before heading out the door.

Like a gentleman, Blake took her by the hand and led her down the few steps. Once they made it to the bottom, he spun her around, admiring the look she'd put together.

"Mmm. Beautiful!" Blake said, and when his full lips parted into that sexy smile, Cadence couldn't help being drawn in.

"Thanks," she said, smiling.

Blake continued holding her hand as he led her to the truck and helped her in.

"Let's go," Blake said once he was in his seat. His eyes washed over her from head to waist and then he sighed and shook his head before starting the truck. The oversize vehicle roared to life.

Cadence pretended not to be moved by the attention he showered on her. Again she recalled Alana's words. "Have fun" and "ride this…" *No pressure, Cadence.* She peeled her banana and sat back so she could enjoy the "ride."

Chapter 14

If Cadence knew what she was doing to Blake by sitting there eating that banana, she would have stopped. Blake was sure of that. He could barely stay within the lines on the road, thinking about all of the things that a simple bite of a banana suggested. He remembered their kiss and the plump softness of her lips from the night before and adjusted himself in his seat.

Thankfully, she finished her fruit and they had made it to their destination without incident. Hopping out of his truck, he rushed to her side to help her out. Blake reveled in the softness of her skin as he took her hand. Subtly he took in the crevices of her bare shoulders and the lines of her long graceful neck. Her ponytail was pulled tight at the base of her neck, affording him an unobstructed view of her pretty face. Her beauty was so natural that she didn't need makeup. That simple hint of color in her gloss was sufficient. Anything more would have marred her perfection.

Purposely he hadn't told her where they were going. He was testing her to see if she was the kind willing to go along for the ride. He wanted to see if she could trust him to take the lead. He intended to show her a good time.

Blake parked about a block away from the fair. When he led her by the hand to the entrance, her pretty smile brightened the glow of her face.

Cadence gasped, placed her hand on her chest and said, "Oh, a carnival." A nostalgic innocence washed over her as she smiled. "I haven't been to one of these in years!"

"Me, neither," Blake said. "I was out running errands this morning and I drove by it. I thought it would be fun."

Cadence hung her head sideways, "Oh. Thanks. I'm glad I came."

The two stood in line and Blake paid the fee affording them unlimited rides. Cadence looked at all of the games, vendors and rides in wistful wonder.

"We have to get on the Ferris wheel," Cadence said, dragging Blake in that direction.

"Let's go!" Blake said, happy to oblige.

Cadence was like a kid. Blake loved the way she jumped right in, knotting her dress between her legs to get on various rides. Over the next few hours, they had rammed each other in bumper cars several times, rode the Ferris wheel twice, spun on the Tilt-A-Whirl until they were dizzy and won prizes in the shooting gallery and the balloon race. After losing to Blake three times in the water-gun race, Cadence turned her water gun on Blake, splashing the side of his face. As payback, Blake turned his gun back on Cadence, spraying her right above her chest. Dropping her weapon, she ran for cover and bent over laughing.

Now they sat, slowly riding through the tunnel of love. A comfortable silence accompanied them as Blake admired her silhouette. Cadence wore a contented smile, and again, Blake felt proud that he had been the catalyst. Cadence rested her head on Blake's shoulder and he closed his eyes, but then his stomach growled. The rumble broke the silence and sucked the romance from the atmosphere.

Cadence looked up at him and they both cracked up laughing.

"It's time to eat," he said, rubbing his stomach. "You ready to get out of here?"

"Yes. My funnel cake wore off hours ago."

Carrying the humongous teddy bear he'd won for her, they made their way back to his truck. Blake strapped in teddy and then Cadence before getting in himself. From there they headed to the Nautical Mile for a seaside dinner and then sat a while, enjoying cocktails and listening to the live reggae band's serenade under the orange glow of the evening sun.

As the band wrapped up their last set, Blake and Cadence finished the last of their drinks and walked back to the car hand in hand. Although the right thing to do was to take her home, Blake didn't really want to. He took his time driving her back. When they pulled up in front of Cadence's house, Blake turned off the engine and turned toward Cadence.

"Have fun?" he asked. That smile returned, making him a proud man again.

"I had a ball!" Cadence smiled and shook her head. "Bumper cars?" She laughed and tilted her head toward him. "Who would have thought? I'm so glad I came. I needed that."

"Me, too."

Blake sighed. He wanted her to ask him inside. He didn't want to ask and have his suggestion misconstrued. Had this been another woman, he would have been in bed with her the night before. This was Cadence. As corny as it may have seemed, her name was truly like music to his ears. Blake waited for her to make a move. A pregnant silence swelled between them, taking up just as much space as the large teddy bear in the backseat. When Cadence didn't make another move, Blake got out and headed to the passenger side of the car to help her out.

Keeping hold of her hand, he took his time walking to the front door. At the top of the steps, he turned to her, waiting for the invitation that he knew was unlikely. Even if she wanted him, which he knew she did, it was too soon for the likes of Cadence. He would play her way. She was worth it.

Neither of them spoke at first. Facing each other, they held hands. When Blake could no longer stand being that close to her without touching her, he pulled her face to his and kissed her. Then he placed his hand in the small of her back and pressed her body against his. Their tongues danced at a slow warm tempo. As if a fire had been lit under them, the heat intensified and the pace of their kiss increased until the rhythm they created pounded in his chest. His hands roamed her body. She purred. Cadence's hands found their way to the back of his head and pulled him in. Time passed. When they finally forced their lips apart, they were gasping. Collapsing into each other, they held on until their heartbeats returned to a manageable rhythm.

If last night's kiss was explosive, then tonight's kiss was reminiscent of a nuclear blast. Blake's body started to respond. An erection swelled in his pants. It was time to go. He pulled her into him again, letting her feel the effects of her. Grabbing her face, he planted a few, sweet, slow pecks on her wet swollen lips and turned without saying good-night. Blake jumped in his truck, revved the engine and sped off, leaving Cadence right on her doorstep with the teddy bear.

Blake should have seen her inside but couldn't risk a loss of control. That woman had managed to plant herself deep in his system. Blake gave himself credit for leaving when he did. Had she opened that door, he may not have been responsible for his actions. The vision of him carrying her over the threshold and having his way with her had already unfolded in his mind. Cadence was precious goods. It was important that she was handled in the proper way. Soon enough, she would belong to him. Blake was certain of that.

Chapter 15

Blake's week had taken a toll on him, with long days spent in court and busy evenings that stretched far into the night. Blake hadn't reached his bed until well after midnight trying to catch up on emails and paperwork. He was determined not to let his workload spill over into his weekend.

It was his parents' anniversary and the Barrington family's annual backyard barbecue was always scheduled for the afternoon. The weather called for sizzling temperatures and clear skies—even though nothing usually stopped Barrington parties from going down.

It was an all-hands-on-deck affair, according to his mother, Joyce. His father may have been the judge, but Joyce gave the orders around their household.

Blake had just returned from helping his father get the yard set up for the throngs of guests that would show up later. Now it was time for him to freshen up and get ready for the cookout himself.

Selecting a more casual look with a black T-shirt, jeans and black sneakers, Blake finished off with a gold cross. His attire was perfect for riding with his brothers, since they all rode their bikes to the family barbecues. His final addition, a few spritzes of his favorite cologne.

Blake jumped on his new red-and-black Ducati cruiser and fired up the engine. It had been his proudest purchase by far because his brother Drew had input on the design. He planned to take Cadence on a ride sometime before the night was over.

When Blake arrived at his parents' sprawling home in a cul-de-sac with backyards that hovered over canal water from Freeport Bay, he noticed that his brothers had already arrived. Their bikes, along with a few others, blocked the entrance to the Barringtons' driveway. Blake pulled his bike up next to a shiny new hog, got off and slid his fingers across the Harley's sleek body as his mouth twisted with admiration.

"Ay, Drew! Hunter!" he called out as he made his way to the backyard. The brothers greeted him with hand slaps and hugs as if they hadn't seen one another just a few hours earlier. "Whose hog is that?"

Drew poked out his chest. "That would be mine," he said proudly. The brothers laughed.

"Ooh! That's sweet. When did you get it, man?" Blake asked.

"I just picked it up yesterday. Had my eye on it for a while."

"Nice." Hunter nodded.

"You guys coming out to cheer me on at the Indy Grand Prix in a few weeks?"

"Oh, Lord! Those darn races. Drew, I thought you told me you were done with those." Joyce placed her hands on her hips and shook her head. "Lord!" She looked up. "Please don't let my son bang that old hard head of his in this race." With her lips pursed, she shook her head again as she placed a chafing dish on the table. "You boys do me a favor and get the rest of the pans out here and line them up on the table. I want to make sure everything is set before more people start coming."

The men followed their mother's orders, chuckling at her concern. She had scolded them about their bike obsessions since their late teens. They got it honest. The first bike they had ever ridden was a Harley that belonged to their dad. Joyce even had her own helmet and jacket to match.

About an hour later, the yard had filled with family, friends and neighbors. A mixture of jazz and R&B soul wafted through the patio from the speakers. Guests were sectioned off in groups, some under the gazebo, others leaning against the back fence taking in the views offered by the canal, and others were just relaxing at the various tables positioned across the grass.

Blake kept looking over toward the gate, keeping an eye out for Cadence's arrival. He wasn't nervous about her meeting his folks, he was simply anxious to lay eyes on her, wondering what vibrant color she would wear today against her creamy caramel skin. Which sensual floral aroma had she chosen to dot her wrists and shoulders with?

When Blake invited her to attend, she had asked then if it was okay to bring Alana with her. He imagined she'd feel more comfortable with her comrade by her side when it was time to meet his parents. By his normal standards, he wouldn't introduce anyone to his family so soon. He had only been seeing Cadence for a few short weeks. Since then, they'd spoken every single day, went out on a few more dates and spent as many of their nonworking hours together as possible. There was no need to waste time when he knew what he wanted.

A short while later, Cadence arrived, floating through the gate like a goddess in an ivory sundress and gold flat sandals. Several heads turned in her direction. Blake proudly walked up to her and planted a sweet peck on her lips. Cadence blushed.

"Hello!" Alana broke into their isolated world. "What am I, rancid liver? If it weren't for me, you wouldn't know her," she teased, and Blake snatched her up into a brotherly hug.

"Aw, come on, girl. Nobody forgot about you. Come on in. Let me introduce you to my folks." Blake led the way.

His father, Floyd, was in his signature spot standing over the grill with a spatula in one hand and a beer in the other, flipping burgers while he sang along with Kool and the Gang. The song switched to "Love and Happiness," and just as Blake drew near, his mother stepped outside. Floyd pulled her into his arms, singing and swaying to the beat. The guests erupted in laughter. They danced for the rest of the song while Blake took Cadence and Alana around to meet a few other folks.

Blake led them over to where his brother stood near the back fence.

"Hey, Alana! What's up?" Hunter greeted her first.

"What's up, Hunter?" Alana lifted on her toes to accept Hunter's hugs. "Drew," she said as a telling gaze passed between them.

Inquisitive stares bounced between Blake, Hunter and Cadence, and then Cadence gave Alana the side-eye. Alana's only response was a dismissive wave. The group engaged in small talk.

Blake took Cadence by the hand. "Come on so you can meet my parents." He saw nervousness flash across her face as her chest rose and fell in a deep breath.

"Okay."

"No need to be nervous. They are really cool people. My grandparents are even cooler."

Leading Cadence by the hand, Blake presented her through the yard as if he was toting a prize. At the double doors, he stepped aside, allowing Cadence to walk in first. Both of his parents were in the kitchen debating over what to put on the grill next.

"Mom. Dad. I want you to meet someone."

Blake's parents turned to them. A warm smile spread across Joyce's face.

"Isn't she beautiful, Floyd?" she said, tapping his arm.

"Cadence, this is my mother and father, Floyd and Joyce Barrington."

"Hello, Cadence. It's such a pleasure to meet you." Joyce pulled Cadence into a welcoming embrace.

"Likewise, my dear." Floyd nodded and shook her hand.

"It's a pleasure to meet you, as well, Mr. and Mrs. Barrington. Thank you for having me in your lovely home."

"Oh! Anytime, my dear." Joyce clapped her hands together. "Anytime. I hope to see you again soon. Perhaps Blake can bring you over for dinner. This way, we can really get to know each other."

That was Blake's cue. "Oh, Ma! We're going back outside." He looked at his father and stretched his eyes before turning to leave. Floyd chuckled, and his booming laughter filled the kitchen.

"Why did you pull me out of there so quick?" Cadence asked once they were back outside.

"My mother is a fabulous woman, but if you let her, she will talk you to death. Trust me, I was saving you."

Cadence laughed, and Blake tried not to be affected by how the graceful lines of her neck gave in to the draw of her shoulders. He liked the way her full red painted lips framed her pretty white teeth.

For the rest of the evening, as the sun gave way to an auburn sky and then dipped into the star-spangled night, Blake stayed by Cadence's side. When it was late and the last of their guests were leaving, Alana, Cadence and Blake's family were tucked under the gazebo chatting about Drew's upcoming race.

"I can't believe you race," Cadence said. "That's so cool."

"You like bikes?" Drew asked.

"From afar."

"You've never ridden before, right?" Blake asked incredulously.

Cadence shook her head.

"You'll have to let me take you for a ride."

"Maybe one day."

"Tonight!"

"Oh no." Cadence held up her hands in protest. "I couldn't. I have on a dress anyway."

"So." Blake just shrugged. "Just tie it up like last time."

"Last time!" Alana gave Cadence and Blake a sideways glance. "What kind of freaky mess have you two been getting into?"

Cadence clucked her teeth. "Alana!"

"I'm just asking." Alana sat back, chuckling.

"You rode the cruiser, right?" Hunter asked Blake. When he nodded, Hunter turned his attention toward Cadence. "You should let him take you for a quick ride. He won't go fast. Blake knows when to play it safe."

Cadence was still shaking her head. "I don't know. Plus, I don't have a helmet."

"I've got one for you," Blake said rather quickly. He had already planned to steal her away before the night was done. Taking her by the hand, Blake said, "Come on. I've got you."

Cadence rose as if she was being lifted by the air. Drew,

Hunter and Alana cheered as Blake led her out toward his bike.

"Don't do anything I wouldn't do!" Alana yelled after them.

"Yeah!" Drew added as their laughter floated through the yard.

Cadence tied her dress between her legs and Blake carefully placed the extra helmet on her head. He straddled the bike, instructing Cadence to get as close to him as she could. She nestled snuggly against his back. Blake turned the key and the bike rumbled to life. Cadence held him tighter.

"I've got you," he said, loud enough for her to hear through the helmets and over the roar of the bike's engine. "Just hold on tight."

Slowly he backed the motorcycle out of the yard and started down the block at a calm pace. He smiled at the feel of Cadence's face buried in his back. Blake rode around for a while and stopped the bike near a quiet setting at the edge of the marina. By the time he pulled over, he was sure there were lines in his chest from Cadence's firm hold. Leaning the bike on its stand, he exited and helped Cadence out of her helmet. They walked over to a large bolder and sat down. Blake tossed a few pebbles into the midnight water, disrupting the flow of the ripples lit by the moon's light.

"That wasn't so bad, was it?"

Cadence narrowed her eyes at him, but then eased her lips into a smile. "No. It wasn't as bad as I thought."

Blake turned to her, closing in on her until there was just a sliver of space between them. "I told you I would take care of you." He was so close that his lips brushed hers as he spoke.

Cadence opened her mouth to respond and Blake covered it with his. From the moment she walked into his parents' yard, he had been waiting to kiss her like this. Their mouths ravished each other as their hands explored all the parts within reach. Blake pressed his body against hers. He wanted her to feel him. Cadence held him closer. Blinding desire shot through him. The groan that escaped rose from deep in his belly.

Cadence broke their kiss and dropped her head back, panting. Blake swooped in and devoured her neck. She moaned and Blake's erection grew rigid until it felt like steel.

"Come home with me," Blake whispered breathlessly into her neck."

"Blake," Cadence said so lightly he could barely hear her. He felt her breath, its ragged rush as she tried to speak. "Uh!" she moaned again.

Blake wanted her bad but wouldn't push it. He couldn't pinpoint what it was about Cadence that made him want to be the perfect gentleman. When he had her it would be because she gave of herself willingly. Blake kissed her one last desperate time, ending with slow soft pecks on her engorged lips.

"Let's get back," he said, still breathless.

"Yes. Let's do that."

Just to feel her one last time, Blake pulled her into a tight embrace and held her for a few moments. She felt good in his arms and he wished he never had to let her go.

Hand in hand, they walked back over to the bike. Blake helped Cadence into her helmet before putting his on. On the bike, Cadence pulled up to the back of Blake until there wasn't enough space for a strand of hair to settle among them. She held his chest and nestled the side of her head into his back.

Blake looked up toward the sky with hope in his heart, before kicking back the stand and starting the bike. He'd had his share of women and had experienced every kind of relationship, from one-night stands to serious connections, but something in Cadence made him want to be a better man.

Blake turned the bike around and rode back into the night, smiling. Blake would have all of Cadence soon enough. Not just her body but her heart, as well.

Chapter 16

It was almost quitting time and Blake was ready for his evening with Cadence. Leaving a few minutes early, Blake decided to pick up a bouquet of flowers from the gentleman selling them out of a bucket at the corner of Forty-Second Street and Sixth Avenue. He stuck the Chick-O-Stick that he'd purchased for her earlier in the center. Cadence had previously indicated that it was her favorite old-school candy, so he thought it would be the perfect complement to their picnic under the big screen and evening sun as they watched *The Karate Kid* on the great lawn in Bryant Park.

Blake spotted Cadence from halfway down the block, keeping his eyes glued to her swaying hips as she made her way toward him. He pulled the flowers from behind his back and kissed her lips gently.

"Aw, thanks!" Cadence sniffed the flowers and smiled.

"I'll do anything to bring a smile to those luscious lips." His chest lifted.

Blake and Cadence made their way to an open spot on the grass and spread out their blanket. They exchanged stories about their workday until the colossal screen came to life with images and saturated the area with music.

"Oh! Wait!" Blake said, alarming Cadence. "Look inside your flowers."

Cadence cast him an inquisitive gaze before sticking her face in the flowers. When she pulled out the Chick-O-Stick, she threw her head back and laughed. "Oh my goodness! How did you know?" Immediately, she peeled the wrapper off and took a bite, dropping her head back, seemingly taken by euphoria.

Blake laughed. "I remembered you said it was your favorite old-school candy."

Cadence laughed as she chewed, and wrapped her arms around him. "Thank you!" Cadence nestled close to Blake as he sat with his arm resting on one raised knee and the other around her shoulder.

When the movie ended, Blake and Cadence held hands as they meandered through the busy New York City night. Blake was glad that he had decided to drive in today and was even happier that they left the city way after rush hour. They had hit some traffic but nothing like the slow drudge that would have crippled their commute a few hours before.

Blake had held her hand through most of the ride home and now that he was sitting in front of Cadence's house, he didn't want to let it go. Like the gentleman that he was, Blake got out, helped her from the car and escorted her to the front door.

Just as he was about to kiss her good-night, she held a finger to his lips. The look in her eyes was smoldering. Blake's groin responded to the penetrating stare and the soft touch of her finger. He took a deep breath in an attempt to get his longing in check.

"I want you to come inside." Her whisper was thick.

Blake swallowed and cleared his throat. "Are you sure?"

"Yes." She looked directly into his eyes.

Blake's core tightened. Involuntarily he licked his lips, lowered those hooded eyes as they journeyed from her beautiful brown eyes, pouty lips, perfect mounds, curvy hips to the center of her thighs.

"Open the door," Blake ordered. Cadence obliged instantly.

Blake picked her up and carried her over the threshold in his arms, never breaking his piercing stare.

"Where to?" Blake asked on the other side of the door.

"Wherever you'd like." Cadence batted her eyes and Blake felt a twitch in his groin.

Blake found his way to her bedroom. He'd been waiting for this opportunity.

"I've been waiting for you," he said. His voice was loaded with desire.

Blake had literally dreamed of making love to Cadence. Placing a handle on his craving, he vowed to take his time. He wanted this first time to be just right. Something they could savor in each other's absence. Careful not to apply too much pressure, Blake lowered himself over Cadence and gave her the lightest kiss.

"Thank you," he said, kissing her. "For trusting me." Kiss. "With your body." Kiss. "I'm going to take my time with you…" Kiss.

A gasp so sweet to Blake's ears escaped Cadence's lips that he wished he could have captured it to treasure later. The rising temperature between them warmed his neck. He reveled in how his words had affected her. Cadence squirmed underneath him and he longed to fulfill her yearnings.

Blake teased her with another kiss, licked her sweet lips and captured her mouth all in an instant. Her kiss felt like the flow of fresh springs after a trek across the desert. He couldn't wait to enter her. True to his word, he planned to take his time, exploring every inch of Cadence. Her pleasure was his priority.

Starting with her lips, Blake traced a moist trail of kisses all the way down to her feet, slowly removing any piece of clothing hindering him from getting next to her supple skin—at last doing away with her shoes. Blake repeated his path of kisses again. He admired her natural glory, exhibiting his adoration by running his hand across the lines of her neck, breasts, stomach and thighs.

Blake carefully removed his clothes. Holding himself over her, his gaze met hers again and he winked. After another greedy kiss, he watched Cadence as she watched him. Lowering to her perfect mounds, he teased each nipple before taking one in his mouth. Careful not to give one more attention than the other, he went back and forth between them, tweaking, sucking and pulling until they stood firmly at attention. Her groans were like his cheering squad, egging him on. He flicked his tongue, discovering and revisiting the ways that generated the most response. Cadence's back arched and Blake could hear a moan start in her belly.

He explored the depths of her navel before sinking his face between her thighs. Parting her legs, he continued to plant tender kisses around her hairless folds before dipping his tongue into her center. Cadence gasped and her back arched hard and high. With the flat of his tongue he toyed with her bud, gently took it between his teeth and teased it. Then he covered it with his lips and lapped until she cried out his name.

Hearing his name from her mouth in a cry of ecstasy was a beautiful serenade. He feasted on her until she convulsed and scampered from his reach, panting his name in rapid succession. When the quivering in her legs ceased,

Cadence reached for his erection and took him in. The guttural sounds emanating from Blake surprised him. He bit his bottom lip trying not to go over the edge too quickly.

Pulling himself from her warm lips, Blake sheathed his erection and slowly pressed it between her folds. Her cushioned canal tightened around him. He felt himself become even more rigid and was rendered immobile for one glorious moment. Moving deliberately so that he could savor the feel of her and defer his excitement, Blake pressed deep, long strokes into Cadence. They rode that way until their pleasure intensified into fiery blasts shooting through their bodies. Groping for each other, they filled the room with the sounds of their ecstasy, collapsing into a crumpled mound of mingled, satisfied bodies.

As Blake floated back to full consciousness, he hoped that Cadence would always remember this because he knew he would never forget.

Chapter 17

Cadence's alarm clock had been going off, but she thought it was part of her dream—the one where she was still in Blake's arms. Realizing the nagging noise was outside her subconscious, she jumped up and grabbed the clock off the nightstand.

"Oh my goodness!" Cadence leaped out of bed. Her train was scheduled to leave in twenty minutes. There was no way she would make it to work on time.

As she raced around snatching clothes from her closet, she thought of what to tell her boss about her impending lateness. She'd just tell him the truth—that she overslept. Of course she'd leave out part about Blake ravishing her body and leaving her to wallow in the afterglow a few hours before sunrise.

Cadence jumped into the shower, standing still for a moment to let the pulsating water cascade over her and wash away her fatigue. The delicious ache between her legs reminded her of why she had overslept. The remembrance of Blake's skillful hands roving her body and the agile way he satisfied her every whim caused an instinctive shudder to ripple through her. Cadence groaned and licked her lips.

Blake was growing on her. She did a mental list of things that she liked the most about him. He was always the perfect gentleman. He paid attention to the small things. He was considerate. Granted, all of this could have been part of his plot to get her into bed, but Cadence truly didn't feel as if he was just another playboy trying to score. There was more to her and Blake. She could feel it. However things worked out, she'd had fun these past few weeks. Alana would be proud.

Cadence hopped out of the shower, grabbed a towel and ran to her bedroom to get dressed. Her phone buzzed. She had missed a call from Blake. Cadence dialed him back.

"Hey," he greeted. His sexy voice sparked a surge of yearning in her core.

"Hey, yourself," Cadence said. When she noticed that she was twisting her naked frame from side to side, she shook her head and stopped, planting her feet firmly into her plush pile carpet. "What's up?"

"Just checking on you. I had a great night."

"Thanks. Me, too." A sheepish grin warmed her cheeks. "As a result of that great night, I overslept and now I'm running late. I'll have to give you a call back later, okay?"

"Me, too!" he laughed. "Have a good day."

"You, too." Cadence hung up the phone and before returning to her frenzy, she stood for a quiet moment wondering if Blake could possibly be the one. "Slow your roll, sister. It's only been a few weeks. We probably haven't even met the real Blake yet," she said to herself and laughed.

After Cadence dried off, she reached for the remote and turned on the television so she could listen to the news while she dressed. She hoped that the Long Island Rail Road trains weren't running late.

Cadence was slipping into her trousers when the anchor-woman announced in breaking news that Congressman William Banks and a possible ring of other politicians and business owners were named in an alleged scandal involving his nonprofit organization, Billy's Promise.

Reaching across the bed for the remote so she could turn up the volume, Cadence looked up at the flat screen hanging on her bedroom wall. A picture of Congressman Banks and four other men filled the screen. Then the broadcaster said something about misappropriated funds and his last campaign. Cadence wasn't sure if she'd heard correctly because of what she'd just seen on the screen. Her hand went limp and the remote fell, crashing to the floor. She covered her gaping mouth as she stared into Blake's face. He was being named as part of Banks's alleged ring.

Instantly, Cadence's face was flush with anger. How could she have possibly fallen for someone trifling enough to take part in a political scandal?

"Oh my goodness!" Cadence covered her face. She took several deep breaths to regain her composure.

A gang of possibilities flooded her mind. *Maybe he's innocent. Maybe he's not.* What would she say to him the next time he called? She couldn't date a man like him? What would her father think?

Cadence held up her hands as if she was telling some-one to wait. "Hold on, Cadence." She reeled herself in. "You're a lawyer. You know how the media can blow things out of proportion." She didn't want to crucify him prematurely. He deserved a fair chance at communicating his side of the story.

Cadence plopped down on her bed. For a moment, she thought about just calling in. She needed time to process what she'd just seen on TV. Blake had really made an im-

pression on her. No. Not an impression. She was falling
for him—hard! She had given herself to him. Nonethe-
less, integrity, honesty and character were uncompromising characteristics for the men she dated. If Blake had the
potential to be this scandalous, wouldn't she have seen the
signs? Blake could be innocent or guilty.

Cadence remembered that Blake had shared with her
that Congressman Banks was his mentor and the founder
of that organization he worked with. Maybe he was guilty.
Maybe Banks was teaching him his scandalous ways. She
had to end this thing with Blake immediately, but would
that be fair? Being an only child, she knew what it felt
like to feel alone. She wouldn't want him to feel that way.
As a lawyer, she knew what it was like for a client to be
prosecuted by the public before having a chance to prove
his innocence.

Cadence hoped he was innocent but knew his reputation could be permanently stained because of this. Could
she afford to continue dealing with Blake when she was
at a critical point in her career? Was she being selfish for
even thinking this way?

Cadence shook her head violently. This was too much—
especially after the things he had done to her body just
hours before. She could still feel his touch. It still affected
her, causing her core to clench. Why this now? Why him?
Most important, what was she going to do about it?

Cadence's phone rang again. Seeing Blake's number
appear, she sent the call to voice mail and silenced her
phone. She couldn't speak to him now. Did he even know
that his face was being plastered across television screens
throughout the metropolitan area—maybe even the entire
country? Angst churned in her stomach.

Still half dressed, Cadence picked up her phone and
tapped out an email to Adam explaining that she was running late. Then she sat back down on her bed staring out

at nothing in particular as the television droned on in the background. It was times like these that she wished she could reach out to her mother. A single tear quietly rolled down her cheek. Cadence didn't even bother wiping it away.

Chapter 18

"Have you heard?" Hunter asked frantically.

It took a few moments for Blake to answer as he paced around his living room couch. "Yes. How the hell could this have happened?" he finally said and flopped down on the black leather couch. The material squeaked under his weight as he dropped his head against of the back of the couch. "How did you hear about it?"

"I got an alert on my phone when I came up from the subway. Have you spoken to Mr. Banks?" Hunter asked.

"I've called several times and I keep getting his voice mail. On top of that, I get a message that his mailbox is full and I can't leave a message."

"Text him!" Hunter ordered.

"Don't you think I did that?" Blake's frustration was getting the best of him. "I'm sorry. I know you're only trying to help. I tried everything—even called his office number and I'm not getting any answers."

Hunter's groan barreled through the phone. "Something

has got to be done. He has to clear your name. You had nothing to do with this, right?"

"Hunter!" Blake admonished. "You know I'd never do anything like this—and ruin the Barrington name. Dad would crucify me."

"I'm sorry. I know you wouldn't." Hunter grunted. "This is bad. Real bad."

"Who are you telling?" Blake heard a beep indicating that another call was coming in on his cell phone. He prayed it was Cadence. Ever since the breaking news hit moments ago, he'd been trying to call her, too, but each call went unanswered. Blake looked at the number of the second caller. "Hold on, Hunter. That's Drew. I'm going to add him in." Blake tapped the phone, merging the calls. "Hunter? Drew?"

"I'm here," they said simultaneously.

"Blake! What the heck!" Drew's voice had risen. "You're innocent, right?"

"Of course I am!" Blake huffed.

"Sorry." Drew apologized. "What are we going to do?"

As upset as Blake was, he could appreciate his brothers' concern and the fact that they always had his back.

When Blake heard the anchorwoman's voice as she announced the alleged scandal, he was surprised to hear that Congressman Banks was at the center of it. The shock of seeing his own face on that television screen had rendered him immobile. Blake stood frozen, mouth gaping for several moments before backing up to the sofa to sit before his legs gave out.

How had this happened? Blake and his brothers loved adventure but would never do anything illegal. They took great pride in being Barringtons. His father had worked too hard at building his business from the ground up for them to compromise their name. Blake couldn't imagine how he could possibly be implicated in any kind of scandal.

"The media have your picture blasted across the screen of every news station in the city. How can we stop that?" Drew asked. His annoyance was resident in his tone.

"We can't." Hunter sounded more defeated than Blake at this moment.

"I have to somehow prove my innocence and get my story out there to combat what the news is currently saying. But first I need to get in touch with Banks and find out what's really going on."

"Call us back as soon as you hear from him."

"Okay. I will."

"In the meantime," Hunter interjected. "We need to get to work on clearing your name. I'm just around the corner from the office. I'll call you when I get up—oh no!" Hunter suddenly changed his tone.

"What?" Blake asked, feeling his heart beat a little faster.

"What's going on?" Drew added.

"The media has the front of the building covered."

"Damn!" Blake yelled, balling his fist tight. "I can't believe this."

Blake could hear the frenzy through the phone as Hunter got closer to the entrance of their downtown office building.

"No…excuse me, please…no… I have no comment," Hunter responded to the barrage of media inquiries.

Blake could picture scores of reporters shoving microphones in Hunter's face, hungry for a morsel they could feed to their ravenous public. He imagined them tossing skeptical glares as Hunter swatted at their questions with "no" and "no comment." Picturing how Hunter had to press through the crowd to get to the door made him shake his head. Their office phone would be ringing off the hook for the rest of the day or longer until this whole thing died down.

"Ugh!" Blake grunted. Suddenly the commotion sounded distant. "You made it inside in one piece?"

"Barely." It sounded as if Hunter was winded. "You'd better stay home today. I don't think it's a good idea for you to show up here. I'll take care of everything on this end."

"You're probably right. I need to make some calls so I can start getting to the bottom of this situation anyway."

"You guys keep me posted and let me know if there's anything you need me to do," Drew added.

"I'll check back with you in about an hour," Hunter said. Each of the brothers agreed, but no one hung up. Hunter finally broke the heavy silence. "It's going to be fine, Blake."

"I sure hope so. Talk to you two later," Blake said and ended the call.

Dropping his head back on the couch once again, he huffed and shook his head. He tried to think of all the scenarios that could have led to such an outcome but kept coming up blank. Blake dialed Bank's number again. There was still no answer.

Next, he made one of the two calls he dreaded. His father picked up right away, but from the cheerful sound of his voice, Blake could tell that he didn't know.

"Dad." Blake's voice nearly cracked under the weight of his respect for his father. He dreaded having to tell him about the alleged scandal but was thankful that Floyd would get the news straight from him as opposed to hearing it from one of the morning broadcasts.

"What's wrong, son?"

Blake took a deep breath and shared the bad news with his father, including the fact that the media had already been camped out in front of the office by the time Hunter arrived at work.

Floyd paused for a long time after Blake told him what he knew so far. Blake didn't know how to take his father's silence and had practically held his breath the entire time.

"I know you're innocent, son. Your mother and I raised you right, so you don't have to convince me. Understand this—politicians and the media can be tricky. I know you have a great relationship with Banks, but until we have all the details, I'd suggest you keep your communications and engagement with him at a minimum. I'm not suggesting that he's guilty, but my first concern is you and your career. Let me make a few phone calls and see what I can find out."

"Thanks, Dad." Blake felt a small sense of relief. So far, his family was in his corner. "What about Ma?"

"I'll explain things to her."

"You think she'll be disappointed in me?"

"Of course not! Now, I can't say she won't be worried."

"I know."

"Okay, son. I'll call you back after I've made a few calls. I still have a few eyes and ears out there."

"You're still sharp, old man." Blake teased his father, which brought on his first smile since he learned about the scandal.

"Sharp. Yes. Old… I don't think so." Floyd and Blake shared a laugh before ending their call.

Blake dialed Cadence's number again. Again there was no answer. Worried, he tried several more times, hoping that there was a slight possibility that, like his dad, she'd missed the morning news. He wanted to be the first to tell her. Something told him he wasn't so lucky. Since the first week he'd taken Cadence out, she'd never ignored his calls, but he could tell by the shortened rings that she was directing his calls to voice mail.

Blake decided to leave a message this time, hoping that she would at least listen to it. "Hey, Cadence! It's me, Blake. I'm sure that by now you've seen the news or have somehow heard about what's going on…" He stopped to take a breath and gather his thoughts. "I want you to know that I'm…" He paused again, wishing he didn't have to make this call. "I didn't do the things that the news is saying. I can't believe this is even happening. Call me when you get a chance." After another silent moment, Blake added, "Please."

Blake ended the call and tossed the phone aside on the sofa. Taking the remote, he turned down the sound on the TV and simply sat for some time watching the silent images. He tried to think of how he could have possibly gotten into this predicament. Without speaking to Banks, he didn't even know how to start to try to clear his name.

Hours passed and he had less than twenty percent battery life on his phone after the constant calls from his brothers, father, Alana and the president of the NYAA. After all this time, he still hadn't heard from Congressman Banks and he was still in the dark about how he was even named as a part of this debacle. What was equally troubling was the fact that he hadn't heard back from Cadence, either.

Though it had been less than sixteen hours since he'd seen her, it felt like much longer. He missed Cadence as if she were a thousand miles away. He promised himself that he wouldn't let it end like this. Blake needed to speak to her, hear her voice and not the one recorded to greet callers on her voice mail. He longed to see her face. Blake wanted to explain to her that he wasn't capable of doing the things that the news had been reporting all day.

Sighing again and feeling as if he'd done more of that in the past six hours than anything, Blake sat down in his home office and fired up his computer. Instead of going crazy trying to get answers that evaded him, he figured he would get some work done. Maybe if he could get his mind focused, he wouldn't think about how this situation could ruin his life. Maybe—just maybe—it would help get his mind off the fact that Cadence didn't want to speak to him.

Blake didn't blame Cadence for avoiding his calls. He understood that a woman like her valued a man with integrity. He'd just have to find a way to show her he was still that man.

Chapter 19

Cadence hadn't expected to be this busy at work. Messages were filling up both her cell and office phones. When she had a moment to sift through her phone log, she found Alana's, her father's and Blake's names among the long list of countless missed calls, but had yet to call any of them back. With all the meetings with Adam and her fellow attorneys she attended throughout the day, she barely had time to think about the situation with Blake. Thoughts of him crept up on her, but her plate was too full to entertain them for more than a few minutes at a time. She was happy for the distraction, which gave her little time to focus on the circumstances.

Amy knocked on her door one more time and then peeked in without waiting for an invitation. "I copied those files you asked for."

"Great," Cadence said, shuffling folders of previously copied files. She put them aside to make space for the handful of files that Amy was bringing to her desk. "Put those over here," she said, tapping the space she had just cleared. "I think with this, we are all done. Wait! Where are the McLennan files?"

"I've already delivered them to Kerry," Amy replied.

"Okay, good. What's she up to?" Cadence asked. Surprisingly, Kerry had kept her distance lately. Cadence wasn't sure if it was because she was no longer seen as competition or if she was bogged down with work. Either way, Cadence hoped it would remain that way at least for now.

"I don't know. I haven't heard a peep from her. I kind of expected her to be prancing around the office, showing off her new title, but she's been surprisingly distant."

"The less I see of her, the better, so that's fine with me." Cadence and Amy shared a laugh.

"Yeah! Her old assistant said she's not easy to work with."

"Ha! You don't say." Cadence and Amy shared another quick chuckle.

"It's been crazy today," Amy said. "I'd better get back to work." Just before walking out the door, she turned back and look at Cadence for a moment before adding, "Let me know if you need anything."

Cadence nodded and answered her cell phone.

"Hey, girl," she greeted Alana.

"How's it going?"

Cadence took a deep breath and released a slow loud exhale. "I don't know. I've been so busy with meetings and transferring files. There are a lot of changes going on here."

"How's the nemesis?" Alana said, referring to Kerry.

"She's been uncharacteristically quiet."

"Really?"

"I'm surprised."

After a few beats, Alana broached the subject. "Have you spoken to Blake yet?"

"No." Cadence offered no additional information. The subject was too tender right now. "Alana, it's a little crazy here. I'm going to have to call you back."

"Cadence!" Alana admonished. Cadence sighed and dropped her head as Alana continued, "Blake didn't do this. He's not that kind of person."

"How do you know?"

"Because I do!" After another beat, "Just call him back...one time...hear him out."

Cadence didn't have to ask how Alana knew that she hadn't answered any of his many calls. They were friends. Surely she had spoken to him—probably encouraged him, letting him know she was still in his corner, as a real friend should. Cadence huffed. "I'll call him tonight after work," Cadence said, though not sure if she actually would, but now wasn't the time to get into that with Alana. She had too much work to do and couldn't afford to allow these thoughts and feelings to have free rein right now. That potential avalanche of emotions would have to be held back until she was in the comfort of her own home.

"You need to. The last thing he needs right now is for those who should be in his corner to abandon him. I know this may not be easy for you, but don't convict him before you hear him out. Okay, sweetie?"

"Okay." Cadence fell silent once again. "Hey, look. I have to go. I'll call you later." Cadence wasn't sure if she would follow up on that comment, either. It was obvious that Alana was still on Blake's side and that made her feel guilty and even more conflicted.

Cadence ended the call and buried herself in work for another hour. Just as she was about to get up and head to the conference room to meet with a fellow attorney to review more case files, her phone rang. This time it was her father.

"Hey, old man," she said, trying to force a smile into her voice.

"Sweetheart!" His endearing tone let her on to the fact that he knew something was wrong. Lewis was a senator; of course he had his finger on the pulse of politics, but after recently meeting Blake, she wasn't sure what he had to say about what was going on. "That fellow that you introduced to me last week, he's the same guy on the news, isn't he?"

"Yes, Dad." Hearing her admit that Blake was involved made the situation less surreal, causing a slight tightening in her chest. This thing was really happening.

"And where did you meet him again?"

"At an event for the New York Association of Attorneys. He's on the board and he's a good friend of Alana's." She was surprised at her own need to defend his character.

"How long have you known him?"

"Several weeks."

"Well, I know that you're a grown woman these days, but I think you need to keep your distance from this young man. That's not long enough to know everything you need to know about a person. Maybe we need to start running background checks on these people. I wouldn't want you to—"

"Dad! Everybody is saying he didn't do anything."

"The media seems to think differently." His tone was firm.

"I understand that, Dad." Cadence softened her tone to indicate to her father that she wasn't trying to challenge him.

"Sweetheart." Cadence could hear his anxiety through the phone. "I just don't want you to get caught up with someone who can't be trusted. You're my only child.

You're all I've got." Cadence nodded her head, familiar with this very sentiment. "This is serious, and I don't want to see you hurt. These political scandals have a tendency to grow legs, drag other people into situations and bring them down. You've got a lot going for you, and now you're talking about pushing harder to make partner or possibly start your own practice." Lewis groaned. "Darn it!" Cadence flinched when he raised his voice. "You're the daughter of a senator, for Christ's sake! We don't need this mess landing at our front door."

"Dad! I know. As you said, I'm a big girl. I can handle myself."

Lewis sighed. "I just worry about you, sweetheart."

"I'll be fine. I have to go. I'll call you later, okay? Love you."

"I love you, too. And stay away from that man," Lewis added as Cadence pulled the phone away from her ear to end the call.

Dropping the phone on her desk, Cadence's shoulders slumped as she rested her head in her hands. Alana was right. She should at least speak with Blake to hear him out. On the other hand, her father wanted her to stay away from him, and she completely understood his point of view. She always listened to her father. Cadence was torn. She wanted to cut ties with Blake, but her heart wasn't ready to let him go so easily.

Chapter 20

Blake found himself pacing yet again on what he felt like was the longest day of his life. The seconds crept into minutes, which crept into hours, stretching his agony out before him. The sun had finally tucked itself into the night and he was still none the wiser about how he had managed to land in this vat of scorching water. According to Hunter, the reporters had camped out in front of his office well into the evening. Another group camped out in front of Banks's office, as well. No statements had been released from Banks's camp combatting the accusations.

Even after all the calls his brothers and father made on his behalf, they still acquired no additional information. He had to speak with Banks. Despite his father's warnings to avoid communication with him, Blake called the congressman's cell phone.

"I'm at the door."

"What?" Blake thought he heard him wrong. "Whose door?"

"Yours. Open up."

Blake trotted to his living room window and peeked through to see if it was really him. Swinging the door open, Blake looked past Congressman Banks and quickly scanned the street. He was alone.

"Come on in." Blake urged him into the house by grabbing his arm. Sweeping his eyes up and down the street one last time, Blake closed the door and led Banks to the living room. Without another word, he walked to the kitchen and returned with two snifters of scotch. Nodding his head toward the sofa, he indicated for Banks to sit before passing him the drink.

Banks knocked the contents of the glass back in one gulp. "Ah." He scrunched his face and tightened his lip before placing the glass down on the teak coffee table.

Blake still held his drink in his hand. Taking a small sip, he placed his glass down, as well. "What the hell is going on?" Blake sat leaning forward with his elbows on his knees.

"I've been trying to figure out where this came from all day."

"Is there any truth to what they're saying about the organization and the campaign funds?"

The congressman's loud grunt gave Blake the indication that there was some truth to it. After a long pause, Banks finally said, "It's complicated."

"What!" Blake stood so fast it took a moment to realize he was on his feet. He began pacing again, his hands on his head. "How much of it is true?"

"Not the part about you, of course. I'm not sure how you were named."

"You've got to tell them I'm not involved. My reputation is at stake here. This is all over the news, every station. Reporters are camped out at my office. I can't even work. I have major cases going on right now. This could be a blow to my credibility as a lawyer." Blake stopped himself, finding his voice climbing higher and higher. He sat back down, took another sip of scotch and closed his eyes. He needed to calm down and think.

"I know! You think I wanted this to happen? I'm going to get to the bottom of this ASAP. My team is preparing a statement as we speak. It will go out to the media first thing tomorrow morning."

"Does that statement say that Blake Barrington had nothing to do with this? Because, if not, then none of this helps."

"Blake!" Congressman Banks stood. "I understand that you're upset. You've always been like a son to me. I never meant for you to be caught up in any of this. I will do everything in my power to make sure your name is cleared, but I don't have to tell you that you'll have to be prepared to fight for your name, as well."

Blake sighed and shook his head. "I know." He got up again, unable to remain still. Pacing helped him manage the nervous energy that coursed through him. "What about the other guys? Are they innocent, too?"

"I made a few bad choices. Unfortunately, other people were caught up in them. Those men are not bad people."

"How did they even get our names?"

"I'm not sure yet. But I promise you I'll get to the bottom of this."

Blake walked over to the window and stuffed his hands in his pockets. "Did my father speak with you?" He spoke to Congressman Banks but kept his focus on the window.

"I see that I received a call from him earlier. I'll reach out to him tonight."

Blake turned when he felt Banks's hand on his shoulder. Turning slowly, he took his time making eye contact with him.

"I promise you, I'll get to the bottom of this." Blake

saw the sincerity in Banks's eyes but wasn't feeling very hopeful.

"I sure hope so. I have too much at stake." Blake thought about his family's practice and his reputation, but what he feared most was losing his chance with Cadence. The thought of her made him drop his head.

Blake walked the congressman to the door.

"I'll keep you posted," Congressman Banks said. "In the meantime, get your team together and get your statement prepared. Don't be afraid to tell the truth."

Blake wasn't sure how to take that but nodded in agreement anyway.

"Oh!" The Congressman stopped in his tracks as he stepped through the door. "If you need me, call me on this other number. Do you have your phone?"

Blake pulled out his cell phone and tapped in the number the congressman relayed to him and then watched as he trudged down the walk and entered a black SUV on the passenger side. He continued watching as the SUV pulled away from the curb and made its way down the dark quiet street until he could no longer see it. For a moment, Blake felt sorry for him. As solid and intimidating as Banks's large frame could be, Blake could see the fear in his eyes. They all had plenty to lose if this situation wasn't cleared up right away.

Blake looked down at the cell phone in his hand and decided to try Cadence's number one last time. He'd already left several voice messages and a few texts. She hadn't called him back yet, but he knew she just needed a little time. Going through the entire day without hearing her voice felt foreign to him. Blake began to look forward to their frequent check-ins. He'd always find something to say to make her laugh. Those were proud moments that he wanted to get back to.

Blake dialed Cadence's number and found himself holding his breath waiting for her to answer. She didn't. Trying his luck, he dialed one more time. Still no answer. His shoulders drooped and he stuffed the phone into his back pocket.

Knowing sleep wouldn't come easy, he decided to take a long hot shower hoping it would wash away some of the tension in his muscles. Blake stood under the pulsating stream of the shower letting the water beat against him until his hands shriveled up like raisins. His tired body barely had enough strength to lift the washcloth and soap, but he pushed through anyway. His mind, on the other hand, was wide-awake, with racing thoughts that had no clear destination. He felt as if he'd been blindsided.

Finally, he got out of the shower and dried off. Tossing the towel over the shower door, he carried his weary body to his king-size bed and lay on his back, letting the cool breeze from his ceiling fan lap at the steam rising off his skin. He was so caught up in his scrambled thoughts he barely heard his cell phone ringing.

Blake got up and reached for his phone. When he saw that it was Cadence calling, he snatched the phone, swiping quickly to answer before the call went to voice mail.

"Hello!" he rushed.

"Hi."

Cadence's voice was soft, timid sounding. For several moments, the silence spoke volumes.

Blake cleared his throat, being the first to break the silence. "Thanks for calling me back."

"You're welcome. What did you want?" Her tone was cordial, borderline cold.

"Cadence…" There was pleading in his voice.

"You don't owe me any explanations." Silence settled in again. "I just want to know—"

"I didn't do this," Blake interjected. "I don't know how

my name got into the middle of it. Banks came to my house tonight to apologize."

"I see."

"Cadence. Can we—"

"Blake," she interrupted him. "Maybe we should take a break until this thing blows over."

Blake's eyes closed as he exhaled. His free hand tightened into a fist. It was as if his muscles instinctively responded to Cadence's words. This wasn't what he wanted to hear. Their distance was already killing him slowly. "Is that what you really want?"

Cadence didn't answer. Blake found hope in her silence.

"It's been a long day," she finally said.

Blake knew this was her way of setting up her goodbye. "Yeah."

"Can we talk later?"

"Sure. Whatever you want," he said, and he meant that. He agreed that they should talk later because then maybe he could think straight and say all the right things. Right now, too many varied thoughts were jumbled in his mind and he wanted to be able to focus when he spoke to her. Contrary to what she said, she did deserve an explanation and he wanted to give her one. As for now, he was just happy to hear her voice.

"Okay." That was her goodbye.

Blake wasn't sure if she heard him say good-night. Plugging his phone into the charger, he lay back down on his bed, eyes following the circular motion of the fan. Sleep still wouldn't come easy, but at least she'd called. One way or another, he'd work his way back into her good graces. He had to.

Chapter 21

Despite a gross lack of sleep, Blake got up before dawn with vigor. It was time for him to take action. If Congressman Banks was going to make a statement, then so was he.

In spite of the early hour, he dialed his brother Hunter. He had to call him two more times before getting an answer.

"What?" Hunter's groggy voice rumbled.

"I'm coming in today."

Hunter cleared his throat. "I don't think you should do that. I told you yesterday, we have everything at the office covered. The media are going to hound you."

"I don't care! I can't sit back and do nothing while watching everything that I've worked for get destroyed. I have a few words for the media anyway."

"Blake—"

"I'm coming in!" Blake declared, interrupting Hunter's protest. "See you at nine."

Before Hunter could say another word, Blake hung up

the phone. Tossing the sateen sheets aside, Blake climbed out of bed and headed for the bathroom. The sun had yet to make its appearance for the day and it was too early for Blake to leave for work, so after brushing his teeth, he opted for a quick run. The coolness of the predawn air was just what he needed to refresh his mind. Once he returned from his run he went to the backyard deck to get in a few push-ups and sit-ups and grunt out the rest of his frustrations with some weights.

By the time the sun rose and sliced its way through his bedroom blinds, Blake was dressed and ready to go. The navy blue pin-striped suit coupled with a light blue dress shirt and stylish tie he chose gave him the camera-ready look he was going for. Hunter had called him several times, but Blake opted to call him back only when he was settled in his seat on the Long Island Rail Road—or the LIRR, as the city's commuters referred to the rail system. No one was going to talk him out of going to work.

Hunter's name and number lit Blake's display once again.

"Top of the morning to you," he said jokingly.

"You're on the train, aren't you?" Hunter asked. Blake could imagine him shaking his head.

Blake was sure Hunter heard the automated voice announce the stop and destination in the background. "You know it."

Hunter chuckled. "Can't say I blame you. I'll meet you at Penn," he said, referring to Penn Station, Blake's final stop on the LIRR. "We'll ride this out together, bro."

"Let's do it," Blake said.

The brothers ended their call and met at Penn Station as they'd agreed. Hunter, coming in from his brownstone in downtown Brooklyn, had a quick ride on the number three train, which stopped at the Thirty-Fourth Street station along with the LIRR. The two met in front of the ticket stations that listed the tracks overhead and jumped back on the train toward their downtown Manhattan office.

As they expected, scores of reporters clamored at the front entrance of their building. From the corner, Hunter and Blake stopped and looked at each other.

"You're ready for this?" Hunter asked.

"As ready as I will ever be," Blake said, brushing his hands down the front of his suit.

"I'll deal with the media," Hunter said, leading the way. Blake nodded in agreement. They had been here before with clients. Both men knew what to do.

"There he is!" one reporter yelled.

"Mr. Barrington. Can you give us a statement?" A young woman shoved a microphone in his face as they tried to make their way to the building.

Hunter held his hand out as a barrier between Blake and the throng of reporters. With a nod, Blake assured him that he was okay.

"Ladies and gentlemen…" Hunter straightened his tie and confidently addressed their audience. Microphones shot in his direction. Camera lights flashed as all fell silent. You could hear a mouse scratching at the concrete as the reporters waited to catch of crumb from Hunter's mouth. Looking into the eyes of several of the reporters, he began, "I assure you that Blake Barrington had absolutely nothing to do with these absurd allegations. My firm, Barrington and Associates, will be working around the clock to take care of this and I assure you that we will eventually be pressing charges against the person or persons who started these ugly rumors. This is nothing more than defamation. That's all I have for now."

"Mr. Barrington!" someone from the crowd yelled.

"Can you answer a few questions?" the young woman asked, but they turned from the cameras.

Hunter nodded his head politely, and he and Blake tried

to meander their way through the remaining crowd and into the building.

Reporters continued to sling questions their way. "How long have you been working with Billy's Promise? Wouldn't you consider yourself as the face of the organization? Where did the money go, Mr. Barrington?"

Blake handled himself well in front of the cameras, but in reality his stomach was twisted in nervous coils. When they finally made it into the elevator, Blake let his head slip back against the wall and exhaled slowly.

"Are you okay?" Hunter asked.

"Yeah."

"We'll be fine."

"I hope so." Despite holding up in front of the media, Blake's confidence was shaken.

Chapter 22

A few days had passed, but without contact with Blake the time trudged slowly. Cadence had to admit that she'd missed him sorely. The memory of his touch was no longer sufficient and her mind was swirling with the possibility of his innocence. She tussled with the guilt she felt for persecuting him herself, counting her avoidance as the indictment. She thought about calling him numerous times. Every time she pushed aside her reservations, breaking news would announce a new development or she'd pass a newsstand on her way to work and see more damaging headlines about the situation, just like this morning.

More important, her father was adamant about her cutting ties with Blake. Senator Payne continued to insist that she stay away from "that man." Cadence understood that this was his way of protecting her from hurt and possible embarrassment. Like her, Senator Payne was taking in every salacious morsel the media fed to the public. Every local channel aired both Blake's and Congressman

Banks's press conferences with each declaring his innocence. Whether Blake was innocent or not, the media was slowly chipping away at his credibility at every turn.

Cadence had had her fill and had begun ignoring the news. The Blake they described was certainly not the Blake who had jazzed up her life in so many ways.

Despite all the reasons that she shouldn't bother with him, Blake's absence left a gaping void that refused to be filled. Though she sent his many calls to voice mail, there were times when the scandal wasn't loitering at the forefront of her thoughts and she would absentmindedly dial his number. When she realized what she had done, she would end the call immediately. He'd always call back. She'd never answer. Why start something that couldn't possibly serve her well?

Cadence missed his scent and his smile. Secretly she held on to him by reminiscing about the sly way he'd turn a simple statement into a sexy innuendo. Even now, sitting at her desk, she daydreamed about the ways he often made her laugh and the places he had taken her to—physically and mentally. When images of them making love flashed before her, it sent an involuntary shudder down her spine. Cadence shook her head, scattering away the sensations that flooded her along with those images.

Grabbing a stack of files, Cadence shifted her focus. She had work to do and a meeting to prepare for. She checked her watch and jumped up when she realized that the meeting had already started. She was five minutes late. Where had the time gone? As she hurried toward the conference room, she thought about the fact that she'd have to stay late to finish some work that she missed as Blake took hold of her focus. The next day would be spent mostly in court and she needed to be ready.

Fortunately, when Cadence arrived in the conference room, many of her coworkers were still engaged in idle chatter. They hadn't even noticed that she slipped in late. Cadence could feel Kerry's eyes on her, and when she looked over in her direction and nodded, Kerry sported a half smirk in response. Recently, Kerry was more than willing to find ways to remind Cadence that she had beaten her out for the position of senior counsel. Kerry made a big deal about getting high-profile cases or taking the lead on existing cases.

Cadence grabbed a cup of coffee and took a seat. Once the meeting got under way, a few cases were transferred to Kerry. One was for a major longtime client. Delight spread across Kerry's entire face and she smiled at Cadence.

"As the newest addition to the team of senior counsel, I'll be sure to familiarize myself with these cases. I plan to give our clients my all and represent the practice in the best possible way." She spoke to the partners, but her eyes somehow seemed to land on Cadence through much of her statement. "Once again, I'm honored to be entrusted with this opportunity."

Kerry's discourse had all the makings of an acceptance speech at an awards show. Cadence fought the urge to roll her eyes. For the rest of the meeting, she ignored Kerry while fighting to cast out impending thoughts of Blake. After the meeting, she met briefly with her co-counsel on the case for tomorrow. When she returned to her office, she buried herself in paperwork. By the time she got home, it was well after nine o'clock at night.

Cadence kicked off her shoes and dropped her bag at the front door before dragging herself to the kitchen. Standing with the refrigerator door open, Cadence scanned the shelves in search of something to quell the rumbling in her stomach. She put on water for tea and threw together a turkey-and-cheese sandwich. Back in the living room, she flopped onto the sofa and pointed the remote at the television. When the screen came to life, the picture with

Blake, Congressman Banks, the rapper Iconik and the boys from the center stretched across the screen. Cadence remembered Blake showing her the newspaper article on one of their dates. She sighed before shutting the television off. The last thing she wanted to hear were the latest developments damaging Blake and fueling her conflicted emotions. Then, for just a fleeting moment, she thought of how this must be affecting Blake and she pitied him.

"Enough!" She spoke into the room and continued eating her sandwich in silence. The teakettle shrieked and Cadence headed to the kitchen. Just as she filled her mug, the doorbell rang. Cadence scrunched her face and checked her watch. "Who is ringing my bell at nine forty-five on a weeknight?"

When Cadence got to the door and looked out, she pulled back and took several breaths. The bell rang again, followed by a few quick knocks. Cadence ran her fingers through her hair and stretched her neck toward the mirror before pulling the door open. The dejected look on Blake's face made her heart skip. Evidence of sleeplessness showed up in deep tired lines. A weak smile lazily stretched across his lips, but it didn't quite reach his eyes.

"Can I come in?" Blake finally asked after moments of them just staring at each other.

"What are you doing here?" Several emotions flooded Cadence. She felt the urge to pull him into her arms but resisted. She was surprised to see him, perturbed about him showing up unannounced, yet happy that he was standing so close. His dejected appearance did nothing to hide his handsome features.

"I was out riding, trying to clear my mind, and I looked up and found myself in your neighborhood, so I decided to take a chance. You hadn't been answering my calls, but I needed to see you, so I hope you don't mind me showing up unannounced. I won't take up too much of your time." His cordial tone felt foreign to her ears.

Cadence stepped aside, pulling the door open a little more. Blake walked in and Cadence led the way to the living room. The silence that filled the space was deafening. Usually, when she was in Blake's presence, the atmosphere was charged with laughter and sensual energy. Now the air around them felt dense, causing the room to feel smaller.

Cadence sat on the sofa, gesturing for Blake to have a seat on the opposite couch. She watched him crack his knuckles and twist his hands, waiting for him to state his reason for showing up. While his head was down, she surveyed him, taking in the broad masculine lines of his shoulders.

Blake finally spoke. "I didn't do the things that they are saying."

"You told me that." Cadence said because she didn't know what else to say. She wanted to believe him.

"I know." Blake sighed. "I never got a chance to really talk to you and tell you my side. Things were going well with us and I felt that you at least deserved some kind of explanation."

"You don't owe me anything," she said, even though she was anxious to hear his side of the story.

His smile was genuine. "Thanks, but I believe I do. My brothers and I have spent the past few days trying to unravel this whole situation and figure out how I became tangled up in it. Congressman Banks has been a mentor to me for years. I filed the paperwork to start the organization when he came up with the idea to start Billy's Promise. Since then, I've handled most of their legal affairs more so as a favor, only charging for certain services. Then I got involved in mentoring the kids and now we have this great bond. I've literally watched some of them grow up. I have never been involved with the finances of the organization." The look on Blake's face pleaded with Cadence to believe him. "He's been more than a friend to me—at least until now."

Blake fell back against the couch and let out an exasperated breath. "I know one thing for sure," he continued. "I'm sure my extensive involvement with the boys at the center had a lot to do with me being implicated, but I'm doing everything I can to clear my name. We issued a statement a few days ago, but it didn't seem to be enough." Blake released a nervous laugh. "I always wanted to be on TV, but this is not what I had in mind."

Cadence listened intently, desperately wanting to believe him. Deep inside she felt that he was telling the truth, but her father's voice kept creeping up on her, reminding her that she should cut her ties. Cadence kept her mouth shut, not trusting herself to speak. Part of her wanted to comfort the forsaken man that sat before her. She wanted to feel herself in his arms again and let him know that she would support him because she didn't believe he was capable of the things the media said. She wanted to turn back time and continue on the exciting journey that had been derailed by the scandal. The frightened side of her wanted to protect her heart. She wished she could hit a switch and silence her conflicting emotions. She also wished she could quiet her father's voice, warning her to stay away.

Blake continued to reveal how the past few days had taken a toll on him and his family. Cadence only picked up bits and pieces of the one-sided conversation as her thoughts continued their battle. Finally, she heard something he said clearly and injected herself into the conversation.

"Since this is weighing so heavily on your family, maybe you should let another firm represent you. That will take some of the pressure off, and the fresh perspective could be helpful."

Blake pulled and gnawed at his bottom lip. "I don't know."

"You know a bunch of attorneys. Get one of your friends from the NYAA to represent you."

Blake twisted his face at the mention of the organization, so Cadence didn't say any more. After a few notes of silence, he finally said, "The NYAA president asked me to step down from the board until this whole thing blows over."

Cadence's mouth opened, but she didn't say a word. Knowing how much the organization meant to him and the amount of time he put into it made her feel bad. "Oh. I'm sorry to hear that."

Again, Cadence's conscience pricked at her. It appears that everyone had already convicted Blake. Neither of them spoke for several moments.

Finally, Blake stood, releasing another breath. "I should be going."

Cadence stood to her feet. She needed him to go, but she wanted him to stay. "Yes. Thanks for stopping by," she said in that same cordial tone that felt awkward. Less than a week ago, he'd taken her to new sensual heights within a few feet from where they currently stood and now she was speaking to him as if he were practically a stranger.

Though he alluded to the end of his visit, he had yet to move. Cadence started toward the door in hopes that he would follow. He did. At the door, he stopped just before walking through. Catching Cadence off guard, he stepped to her, leaving only a smidgen of space between them. Cadence could feel the heat of his exhale. The scent that she missed so much filled her nose. Her breath caught. She had been looking down. Finding the courage to lift her head, she stared into his eyes. Beyond the forlornness, she saw desire. Blake's narrowed gaze burned through her. She stood straight and closed her eyes, resisting his effect. She knew that at any moment she would feel his lips against hers and wasn't sure if she would protest. She missed his kisses and recalled how weightless she felt after he devoured her with his mouth, how electricity seemed to flow through her when they connected.

Cadence felt Blake's forehead rest against hers. His strong hands held both arms. She opened her eyes and noticed that his were closed. Blake moved his lips closer to hers but paused just before they made contact. Cadence felt her heart quicken and swallowed the lump rising in her throat. Blake pulled back, released his hold on her arms and sighed. Slowly he turned and walked out the door. Cadence pushed it closed and watched him through the pane as he sluggishly made his way down the walk, mounted his cruiser and sped off. She stood there for several more moments until her breathing returned to its normal rhythm. She couldn't deny the fact that he still affected her. For the sake of her sanity, she had to find a way to get over him—fast.

Chapter 23

Once again, Blake pushed through the throngs of reporters camped outside his family's law offices. The number had dwindled slightly in the past few days, but many still hung around to catch a glimpse of him and push their microphones in his face hoping for a fresh development. When he arrived upstairs, Hunter was in his office engaged in a heated conversation.

Blake leaned against the door frame and waited. He could tell by Hunter's knitted brows and agitated tone that his morning was equally horrible. Blake still hadn't had a full night's sleep and the stress of the situation had now affected his appetite. Worst of all, things were still shaky with Cadence.

Blake knew he was taking a risk by going to her house unannounced last night, but he just had to see her. The sound of her voice lingered with him, tickling his ears. He hadn't made any headway with her by phone and longed to be in her presence. He also needed to feel her out. The distant manner in which she dealt with him confirmed that he had a good chance of losing her for good. He had only hoped his explanation gained some kind of ground.

Hunter ended the call and stood abruptly, steering Blake away from his thoughts of Cadence. "Bad news!"

Blake sighed, readying himself for what Hunter was about to say.

"You should sit." Hunter gestured toward the chair in front of his desk, but he remained standing.

Blake watched Hunter walk back and forth, waiting for him to speak. "Just spit it out, man!" He was losing his patience.

"Banks was just arrested. This is going to take over the news for the next few days." Hunter shook his head.

Blake deflated as if the air was being sucked from him. Reaching for the arm of the chair, he took his time sitting down.

"The attorney general has taken over the case. This means…"

"They found something that they think they can use against him." Blake finished his brother's sentence and rested his head in his hands.

"Exactly! From what I understand, all of his financial records have been seized. I have a feeling they may come and try to snoop around our records since we've received checks from Banks before for legal services."

"You think they are going to try to arrest me, too?" Blake stood, no longer being able to sit still. "Ugh!" Now both he and Hunter were pacing on opposite sides of the desk.

"They shouldn't, especially since they really don't have anything on you other than a couple of pictures of you with Banks and the kids. We've never taken money from Banks, or anyone, for that matter, that wasn't attached to legitimate invoices." Hunter stopped pacing. "Wait!"

Blake stopped pacing, too, alarmed by the nervous tone of Hunter's voice. "Has Banks ever given you money for anything else—payments for something that could potentially look suspicious?"

Blake stood thinking for a few moments. "Not that I recall. In fact, I hardly ever charge him when he asks me to review contracts."

"Whew!" Hunter took a breath. "Then there really shouldn't be anything incriminating in his financial records that points in our direction. We just have to worry about the media. They love a good scandal and can sometimes do more damage than the law. The sooner we can get your name out of this, the better."

The brothers paced in silence for several moments. Suddenly, Blake stopped moving. "I have an idea."

"What?"

Blake thought about Cadence's statement from last night and the fact that their firm's financial records could be subpoenaed. With Banks now under arrest and the attorney general taking over the case, things could really go awry.

"Cadence works for Maco, Dunlop and Norman, one of the largest law firms in the metropolitan area." Blake started walking again. His eyes narrowed as the idea unfolded in his mind. "We'll have Cadence take over the case. Her company has mega clout, for one, and two, it will take the pressure off our firm, especially if the attorney general decides to start rummaging around our accounts."

The look on Hunter's face told Blake that he wasn't keen on his idea. Hunter went to speak, but Blake held up his head. "Just hear me out. Please." Hunter dropped his shoulders and gave Blake a look that encouraged him to continue. "I'm not saying we can't handle this case, but with the AG involved and the amount of publicity the case is getting, it may benefit me to have representation from a legal giant. It can take the pressure off the family and the firm."

At least Hunter was hearing him out. He took that as a license to continue. "Just think about it," Blake pleaded. "We've been consumed by this for the past few days. With Cadence's firm handling my case, you could get back to handling cases for our paying clients."

The more he thought about it, the more he liked the idea. Not only would this help Hunter, who had been working countless hours free, but it would help him get back in Cadence's good graces. What better way to prove his innocence than by having her be directly involved in unraveling the truth behind the allegations? That would force her to be around him—not in the way that he'd prefer, but at least he could get close enough to start chipping away at her stiffened demeanor. He would do just about anything right now to see her smile again.

That last thought stopped Blake in his tracks. The depth of his feelings for Cadence struck him. He wanted her and had already tried to make that clear, but it was at this moment that he realized just how badly he wanted her. Cadence was the woman that he could see himself marrying. She could be the mother of his children one day, and his daughter, if he was really lucky, would be just like her in every way. Suddenly, involving Cadence became even more important. Blake was so wound up in his thoughts that he didn't hear Hunter speaking.

"That's it!" Blake rushed out of the office.

"Blake!" Hunter yelled after him.

"This will be good for both of us," he shouted over his back to Hunter. "I'll be back."

Blake was out the door before anyone could call his name again. Outside, he ignored the reporters clamoring after him as he hailed a taxi and headed to midtown. His mind raced with possibilities. Tossing the driver the fare plus a few extra dollars, Blake got out in a rush and within a few steps found himself inside the polished lobby of the building that housed the Maco, Dunlop and Norman law firm.

Nervous energy coursed through him as he ascended the elevator to the forty-third floor. He felt hopeful. Smiling widely as he got off the elevator, he greeted the receptionist cheerfully.

"Good morning!"

"Good morning to you." The wattage in the receptionist's smile matched his. "How can I help you today?"

"I'd like to see…" Blake paused and decided to change up his strategy a little. "Who does Counselor Payne report to?"

The receptionist appeared to be taken aback. "Well…"

"Not that there's anything wrong. In fact, I think she's a brilliant attorney and I'd like to communicate that to her boss."

The receptionist's eyes shifted away from him and Blake followed her line of sight to the silent flat screen on the wall in the lobby. Congressman Banks was cuffed and being led from his offices. The next image was that of him, Banks and the other two men implicated in the recent charges.

"And as you can see, I have a serious matter for which I'm seeking immediate representation." Blake flashed his best smile before adding, "Right now."

In the most poised fashion, the receptionist nodded. "Sure. Just give me a moment and I'll see if Mr. Benjamin is available."

Instead of calling, the woman disappeared behind mahogany doors. Blake took a seat and tried to channel his nervous energy. His foot shook involuntarily as he thought about how Cadence might react to what he was about to do.

Chapter 24

It was another unbelievably crazy day. Cadence found herself up against a cougar of many sorts. Not only was the opposing attorney known for her proclivity for younger men, but also she was fast on her feet and giving Cadence and her colleague Seth Ferguson a real run for their competencies. Cadence hated being up against her, but secretly admired her fire and tenacity. She made Cadence dig deeper and sharpen her skills. The case presented an unwelcome but constructive challenge. Win or lose, Cadence could see herself walking away from the situation as a better lawyer.

Despite Cadence's clients' strong reputation, there was a good chance that they would have to reach deep into the bowels of their reserve and pay richly for allegedly stealing and profiting from their accuser's ideas after breaching his contract. Now that Cadence and her colleague were done with court for the day, they planned to go back to the office and brainstorm creative ways to gain an advantage over the prosecution. First, they stopped for something to eat and began discussing strategies. Fortunately, they were seated quickly at one of her favorite Italian eateries, not too far from the courthouse.

"I feel like I just got a whipping and then had my wounds licked by my assailant."

Cadence laughed. "I know. Did you see how she winked at you when we were leaving the courtroom?"

"I wasn't sure if she was flirting or if it was one of those I'm-gonna-win-this-thing kinds of wink."

"Ha!" Cadence snickered as she took in a mouthful of pasta. "I think she likes you."

"Pfft!" Seth waved her accusation away. "That woman is almost old enough to be my mother." Cadence shook her head and then Seth paused, bringing his fork to an abrupt stop midway between his plate and his mouth. His pensive look lingered for a moment before he spoke again. "She *is* pretty hot for an older woman," he said and stuffed the fork in his mouth. "Did you check out her legs?" He raised his brows.

"Seth!" Cadence chided.

"What? It's true, but I'd be afraid she'd eat me alive." Seth stretched his eyes. "Literally!" he added.

Cadence held her hand over her mouth to keep food from spraying as she laughed. The conversation moved to strategies for winning their case as they finished their meal. They left the restaurant with renewed faith in their plans and hopped into a taxi en route to their midtown office building.

They were still engrossed in their deliberations when they stepped off the elevator. The receptionist had to call Cadence's name twice to catch her attention.

"I'm sorry. What can I do for you?" Cadence asked.

"Adam would like you join him in the war room upstairs. He said to let you know as soon as you arrived."

"Oh!" Cadence raised her brows, tossing Seth a questionable expression. He shrugged his shoulders. The war room was the nickname for the conference room on the partners' floor where they congregated to debate major cases and big decisions.

"Okay," Cadence said. "If you could please let him know that I'll be right there, I'd appreciate it. I just need to drop this stuff off in my office." Cadence held the files in her hand a little higher.

"No problem," she said.

"Thanks." Cadence nodded.

Cadence walked through the door Seth held open for her. She threw another pondering look at him and again he shrugged, holding his hands up innocently.

As she hurried to her office, Cadence wondered why Adam wanted to see her. She set down the documents in her arms and put her purse away. She took a deep breath before grabbing a notepad and pen. Nervous energy whirled in her chest as she rushed upstairs to the war room. Stopping just outside the open door, Cadence took a moment to catch her breath and stand straighter before entering. Hearing laughter coming from inside calmed her nerves a little. However, when a familiar laugh sparked immediate recognition, every muscle in Cadence's body tensed. Moreover, when she stepped in and her eyes landed on Blake mid-laugh, she thought her legs would give out.

"Ah! Here she is," Adam said as he and Blake stood respectfully. Adam waved his arm in a sweeping gesture as if he had just introduced her to a welcoming audience. "I understand you may already know the firm's newest client, Mr. Barrington."

Cadence responded professionally with a nod and shook Blake's hand before taking a seat on the opposite side of the enormous table, putting as much distance between them as possible. On the inside, she wanted to snatch that proper smile from Blake's face for catching her off guard. Did Adam know just how well she knew Blake? What had he told Adam? Did Adam just say that Blake was the firm's newest client? Why did Blake have to look as handsome as she'd ever seen him? What was going on?

After Cadence sat, Blake and Adam took their seats. Adam began to facilitate the unexpected meeting.

"Cadence, I'm sure you're aware of Mr. Barrington's current situation. It's been all over the news."

"Yes. I'm completely aware." Cadence turned her body toward Adam to keep from glaring at Blake and hoped that she was doing a decent job of keeping the sting out of her voice.

"Well, Mr. Barrington and his firm decided to turn the case over to us—a fine decision, if you ask me." Cadence just smiled and nodded. Adam cemented his confirmation with a nod toward Blake. "After what he has disclosed to me, I don't doubt that we will be able to clear his name and obtain justice for him and his firm. I'm glad that he's chosen us to represent him. Furthermore, Mr. Barrington has requested that you lead the efforts." Cadence's head jerked in Blake's direction. She couldn't help it. Adam continued speaking as if he didn't notice her sudden change of disposition. "I assured him that he's made a smart decision since I believe that you are one of our best associates."

Blake now centered his attention on Adam. He seemed unfazed by Cadence's glare. "I have full confidence that with your firm's reputation and talent I will be able to come through this debacle having my reputation restored."

Cadence couldn't bring herself to speak. Forcing a smile, she clamped her mouth shut to keep her angry sentiments at bay and turned her attention back toward Adam.

"Due to the high-profile nature of this case, I will work closely with you for support. I'll need you to temporarily clear your calendar so that we can give this case our full attention until things are all ramped up."

"Yes, sir."

"Great!" Adam planted his hands on the sturdy table and lifted from his seat. "We'll start first thing tomorrow morning. Mr. Barrington will return at nine with all of the documentation that he thinks will be helpful for us to obtain a successful outcome."

Blake sauntered over to Adam and the two shared a firm shake. "I look forward to it, Counselor."

"You're in good hands," Adam said and then looked over at Cadence and smiled.

Cadence smiled back and picked up her pad and pen. She didn't want to shake Blake's hand, but she was a professional. "You're in good hands, Mr. Barrington," she said with stiffness that she hoped Adam didn't notice. Then she shook Blake's hand. She hadn't counted on the jolt of electricity that surged through her when he touched her. Cadence pulled her hand from Blake's grasp and rubbed her palms on the sides of her legs to stop the tingling.

"I'll see you in the morning, Mr. Barrington," Cadence said as cordially as possible. "Adam." Cadence gave him a courteous nod before walking off.

Cadence couldn't wait to get back to her office. She tried to keep the heaving of her chest at a minimum. Her poker facade was waning and she needed to be alone behind closed doors as soon as possible. Jabbing the elevator button again, Cadence grimaced as she shifted her weight back and forth from one foot to the other. Irritation made her foot tap instinctively. She charged into the empty elevator and stabbed at her floor number. The slow doors seemed to mock her, trying her patience. She poked the button to close the door several quick times. Just as they were about to shut completely, a hand waved between them, causing them to spring open.

Cadence sucked her teeth and then cleared her throat just in case it was Adam. When Blake's body appeared in the opening, Cadence looked around him to make sure he was alone and then glared at him. Blake casually stepped in and stood beside her.

Cadence turned away from him and set a hard focus forward. As soon as the door closed completely, she shot a gaze full of daggers in Blake's direction.

"What do you think you're doing?"

"Just trying to clear my name."

It took several attempts before Cadence could formulate a string of appropriate words. After a deep breath, she continued, "Don't think that I don't know what you're up to, but there's nothing going on between us. This is my job, and since I'm being forced to represent you, it's extremely important that you know I expect you to remain professional at all times!" Cadence wanted to say more, but the elevator had stopped on her floor and the doors were opening. She glared at him one more time before stepping off and not looking back.

"See you in the morning, Ms. Payne," Blake said to her back.

Cadence didn't bother answering. Instead, she marched down the corridor, straight into her office, and slammed the door behind her. With all the anxiety coursing through her, Cadence couldn't sit. She paced, rambling about Blake's audacity and how he'd put her on the spot. She wasn't sure if she was ever going to speak to him again and now she had to represent him. For days, she'd fought the urge to call him just to hear his voice, wishing she could push back the clock and erase the scandalous ordeal so they could continue on the path they started. Now he had sat across the table from her, shook her hand and left it tingling. Inside the elevator, he stood so close that she could smell his natural manly essence as it mixed with his cologne, which tickled her nose as electricity rode the waves of her nerves.

Cadence was angry about being blindsided, but as mad as she was, the sight and scent of him had her reeling. How would she ever get through this case?

She paced for a long while and then finally flopped into her chair. She thought about asking Adam to give the case to another attorney, but she knew that wouldn't sit well with him or the firm. This "client" had asked for her specifically. Additionally, this was a high-profile case and any attorney in the city worth their JD would love to have it in their repertoire. She had no choice but to get her emotions in order and give this case her all. Adam had told her to make it a priority.

There was a light tapping at her office door. Cadence drew in a breath and sat back before saying, "Come in."

The door opened slowly and Seth stuck his head in. His curious expression made Cadence smile a little.

"Everything okay?"

"Yeah." She waved and then nodded.

"Good! I saw how you came charging into the office when you got back from upstairs. I thought you needed a minute."

"There's a good chance you'll have to finish the case on your own or it may get assigned to another team member. I've been placed on a new case and I'll have to meet with the client first thing in the morning. All of my time and attention will be going to that until further notice."

"Wow! Wait! Are you telling me I'll have to battle the cougar alone?" Seth feigned a terrified expression.

Cadence chuckled. "Sorry, buddy. I'm sure you can handle her. I have faith in you."

The two shared a laugh that was abruptly interrupted when Kerry came rushing past Seth. Stunned, they exchanged glances as Kerry charged up to Cadence's desk and slammed her hands down. She leaned into Cadence's face. Cadence reared her head back, putting distance between them while glaring back at Kerry.

"What did you do to get the Barrington case? That case should have gone to me!"

Cadence stood. "Well, Kerry," she started calmly. "I guess you win some cases and you never get a chance to try others. Now, if you'll excuse me, I have a lot of work do to on this very important, high-profile case that I was handpicked for."

Kerry held her glare for a few seconds before retreating. "Very well," she said, and clapped her hands as if she was clearing dust from her palms. "Good luck," Kerry said through tight lips that matched the stiff expression she tossed at Cadence before walking out.

Seth looked from Kerry to Cadence and shook his head. "I'll leave you to your work."

"Thanks," she said and sighed. Now she had even more of a reason to make sure she did her best to win this case. Not only would the public be watching intently, but Kerry, too.

Chapter 25

Blake knew his actions the day before were erratic, and clearly his intentions weren't just about clearing his name and reputation with the public. After speaking with his father and brother when he returned to his office, they helped him realize that his decision wasn't that rash, after all. His father liked the idea of taking the pressure off the family business and getting a major law firm on Blake's side. Maco, Dunlop and Norman had won their share of high-profile cases. What Blake hadn't mentioned was the fact that Cadence would lead the team, per his request. To him that was a major benefit. However, he doubted anyone else would see it that way.

Blake took extra care in preparing for his morning meeting with Cadence. Picking out his best-tailored suit, he matched it with his mother's favorite shirt and tie, hoping that Cadence would like it, too. As much as he longed to see her, he hadn't anticipated the thundering in his heart when he'd laid eyes on her the day before. He didn't care that she didn't appear to be as happy to see him, as long as he was able to be in her presence.

Blake remembered the shock Cadence tried to hide when she stepped into the conference room. It had only been days, but she seemed more beautiful than he remembered. He reveled in hearing the sound of her voice in person, despite the fact that it was drenched in irritation. She was angry, but he knew that in time she would come to understand. Substantiating his innocence to her would be the only way to win her back. It was going to take work and he was ready to put in all the overtime necessary to make it happen.

With more pep in his stride than he'd had in days, Blake grabbed the documents he had compiled and strolled out the door. He felt his confidence returning.

He was eager to start and arrived a half hour early. When the receptionist arrived, she led him to the conference room and offered him a cup of coffee. Blake made use of his time by sorting the files he'd brought with him as he sipped and waited for Cadence to join him.

When he heard her voice approaching the entrance, he smiled. The sound was like a treat to his ears. He stood respectfully as she walked in with another woman carrying an armful of files. He allowed his eyes to feast on Cadence quickly so he wouldn't be caught staring in a way that could be deemed inappropriate.

"Good morning, Mr. Barrington," she said without looking his way. "Amy, this is our new client."

"Mr. Barrington." The young brunette nodded and shook his hand.

"Please call me Blake," he replied with a polite smile and then turned his attention to Cadence. "No need to be so formal."

Cadence cleared her throat. "Let's get started." Cadence proceeded to inquire about the files Blake had brought with him. She followed that up with a thorough list of questions about his alleged involvement with the congressman and his organization. She added this information to the files she and Amy had pulled together. They spent the next few hours sorting documents and planning their strategy.

"It looks like we're in good shape. Now all we need to do is get our hands on the documents the attorney general seized from Banks's office to confirm our argument. Mr. Barrington," Cadence addressed him formally again. Blake tilted his head. "Blake," she adjusted. "Is there anything you can think of that could negatively affect our position?"

Blake thought for a moment and shrugged. "I don't believe so."

"Good. Now, Amy, if we could get copies of all of these files here and here." Cadence planted her hands on top of two large piles. "Then we can give these back to Mr. B— I mean, Blake—and we will be ready to prepare a statement. I think it will be best if we start with another press conference, letting the public know that we are now representing Mr. Barrington, and move forward from there. Are you okay with that… Blake?"

"That's a great starting point. I think it will help show how serious we are."

"Great. So…"

"Cadence?" Amy interjected. "It's past noon. I can order lunch while I'm making these copies. What would you like?"

"That sounds good. Mind if I treat?" Blake offered.

"Thank you but no thank you… Blake. We will take care of lunch. The firm wouldn't have it any other way. Amy, please bring in some menus."

Amy's departure gave Blake his first moment alone

with Cadence since morning. For the first few seconds, he watched her avoid eye contact with him.

"Cadence…" He called her name as softly as he could. He wanted to say it over and over again but resisted the urge.

Instead of acknowledging him directly, she simply paused, keeping her eye trained toward the back of the room.

"Can we talk?" Blake asked.

"All we need to talk about is this case." She continued shuffling papers.

"Cadence." This time Blake stood. He could see Cadence's body become tense when he took a step in her direction. It pained him that his approach would cause her to withdraw. She tried hard not to be affected by him. It wouldn't be easy, but he had to get her to loosen up. He stayed put, allowing her the comfort of her personal space.

"What?" she asked sharply through tight lips.

Amy walked back in the room and Cadence let out a sigh of relief.

"Okay." Amy appeared to be oblivious to the tension in the atmosphere. "I have several menus. We can do pizza, Chinese, Subway or my favorite deli. They have this turkey sandwich on raisin bread that is amazing."

"That sounds good. Can I see that menu?" Blake asked.

"Sure." Amy trotted to his side of the table and handed it to him with a smile. Blake politely smiled back. Blake saw Cadence's expression in response to Amy's smile and averted his eyes. "Think about what you want. I'll check on the copies and will be right back."

"You're the best, Amy," he added.

Amy giggled. "Thanks, Blake."

Blake watched Cadence as Amy left the room. The look on her face told him she hadn't liked the brief exchange.

"Don't flirt with the staff."

Blake chuckled. "You're jealous?"

Cadence sucked her teeth. "Don't flatter yourself."

Blake held his hands up in surrender. "There's only one woman I'm interested in flirting with." Cadence shot him a look that said *don't go there*. "But right now she's not interested in me and I respect that."

Cadence cut her eyes and continued reviewing the document in her hand. "You could have said something to me, Blake," she said with her focus still on the files.

Blake watched her for a few more moments. "Cadence." She sighed and rolled her eyes but didn't turn his way. "I want you to know that I chose this firm and you because I think you're brilliant and I trust that you can get me out of this situation. I believe in my decision to hire your company. It's important that you are part of this process. I just wanted you to know that."

Cadence blinked a few times. "No problem," she said quietly and returned to her files.

Blake had wanted to clear the air. He didn't want her to be so uncomfortable in his presence. He couldn't bear how heavy it made him feel. Soon this would be behind them and she would be back in his arms again.

Blake's attempt seemed to work. The second part of their day felt lighter. Cadence even smiled at one of his silly jokes while they were eating lunch. It wasn't the laugh he used to enjoy coaxing out of her, but it was a start. He didn't miss the sultry line of her lips and the faint smile that framed her mouth. Blake delighted in the feminine curvature of her neck as she twisted and stretched from hours of perusing files. He savored the delicate way her hands moved as she worked. Even more, he respected her diligent way of attending to every detail of the case and the competence she exhibited. Seeing her professional side made him want her even more. Together they would be dynamic. Blake had only hoped that his observation of her didn't become too apparent. He yearned to see the fun, relaxed and passionate sides of her real soon.

More hours passed and it was time to bring their day to a close.

"I must say, Blake. You came well prepared. I think we have enough. I hope that the attorney general's office will get that information from Banks's records to us, and we will be ready for our press conference. I don't want to declare our client's innocence on TV and have something come up on us and backfire," Cadence said as she began clearing the table. "Amy, if you can see if Adam is available, I'd appreciate it. I need to meet with him before I leave here today."

"No problem," Amy said as she reached for the conference room phone.

"I'm glad you're pleased with what I've presented so far." Blake smiled wide, thankful for her and the time he was able to spend in her world.

"We'll give you a call as soon as we hear back from them."

"Great." Blake walked over to Cadence. After sitting across the wide conference room table all day, it was the closest he was able to get to her. He'd been careful to keep his distance. Still, he wanted to get close enough to smell her and would have done anything to hold her hand. "What are you doing for dinner?"

Cadence's head whipped in his direction. "Mr. Barrington." She spoke low, glancing over at Amy to make sure she didn't hear. "Our involvement is strictly professional."

Blake held his hands up in surrender. "Okay." Inside, his heart deflated.

"Have a good night, Mr. B— Blake." Cadence said, and then turned and walked out the conference room, leaving Blake and Amy behind.

Chapter 26

Cadence couldn't get out of that conference room soon enough. When she reached her office, she didn't bother putting down the files in her hand. She simply threw her blazer over her arm and headed for the elevator. She wanted to meet with Adam and get out of the building as soon as possible.

Cadence wasn't even sure how she survived the day sitting across from Blake. As much as she reminded him that their interactions were to remain strictly professional, she found it extremely difficult to focus. Flashbacks of their intimate times together broke her concentration. She tried to ignore the way his glimpses triggered warm sensations in her belly. Her heart palpitated when he licked those luscious lips of his as he spoke. Cadence didn't know if he was trying to seduce her or if she was just taken in by the remembrance of those same lips across her molten skin. Her heart and body were making it clear that she still wanted him. Hopefully, her mind would keep her heart and body in check. In order for her to be successful in representing him, she had to find a way to turn her desire for him all the way off.

Being firm with Blake was her only option. Cadence knew that at times she was being borderline rude, but she had no choice. Breaking down would allow him to get under her skin and she couldn't afford to let that happen. She was still annoyed about how she'd been blindsided. Yet, admittedly, she wanted to know how he got involved in the scandal.

On the train ride home, she thought of numerous ways to handle the case as quickly as possible. Of course, she wanted a winning outcome, but the sooner she could get Blake out of her way the better. She rooted for his innocence. Then there were her father's words. He would see his only daughter and their family's name being dragged through the proverbial mud regardless of whether Blake was guilty or not.

Cadence's mind was brimming with thoughts about the case. She hadn't realized that she reached her stop until the recorded voice announced it a second time. Jumping up, she apologetically leaped over the person seated next to her and ran off the train just before the doors closed. Cadence walked to her car, dropped all the extra files on the passenger side and plopped into the driver's seat. She let out an exasperated breath and sat for a few moments before starting the car.

At the house, she kicked off her shoes, put on a kettle of hot water and headed to her home office. Spreading the files across her desk, she intended to find solutions and formulate her argument. If she had to work all night for the next few days or weeks, she'd do so.

Cadence's vision had begun to blur from hours of perusing documents and staring at her computer screen. She had developed plans for the case. Once she was done reviewing all of Blake and his law firm's files for anything that could be incriminating, she would work with her team to scour the files from Banks's lawyer's office when they arrived. As long as Banks's financial records didn't show any activity that would hinder the case, she could stand before the media and Blake's accusers with confidence.

The chime of her cell phone broke the silence in the room. Seeing that it was her father, Cadence picked up right away.

"Hey, Dad."

"Sweetheart!"

Senator Payne's tone put Cadence on alert.

"Is it true that you're handling that Barrington gentleman's case?"

"How…" Cadence was about to ask how he found out. Her father was a senator and a well-connected former prosecutor and this was a political scandal, so she didn't bother. News traveled swiftly in some circles. "Yes, Dad." She decided to just answer his question and then braced herself for his response.

"I can't tell you who to represent, but be sure to keep your distance. Don't get caught up in the feelings you had for him."

"This is all business, Dad. Don't worry." Cadence hoped she came across as reassuring as she intended. Truthfully, she fought against her feelings for Blake every day. The fight was more grueling with her personal feelings invading her professional space. "Well, I need to put in some more time going over some briefs before bed. How about I call you tomorrow?"

"You do that, honey. Good night."

Cadence jumped back into her work, letting hours roll by as she buried her head in her task. After a long while, she checked her watch and saw that it was after ten o'clock. She had done enough for one night. Tired eyes made it difficult to continue reading. Her phone rang and at first she was going let it go to voice mail but decided to answer the call. When she saw Blake's number on the display, Cadence took a deep breath and let it out slowly. After spending all day with him at the office, her resolve was too fragile to deal with him now. She also thought about her father's latest warning. She let the call go to voice mail and headed up to her bedroom.

Cadence wanted to go straight to bed but figured a shower would help her sleep better. Despite her attempts to push thoughts of Blake from her mind, she pictured his face as she stood naked under the spray of the showerhead. A moan escaped, her eyes closed and her head hung back as she lathered her smoldering skin. She imagined his hands rubbing her down instead of hers but then shook the image from her mind, grunted and shut the water off. Cadence snatched her towel down from the curtain rod and wrapped herself inside the plush softness.

"Come on, girl. Get it together," she scolded herself and sucked her teeth. "He's no longer a contender."

Back in her bedroom, Cadence slipped on a T-shirt and climbed between crisp sheets. Random thoughts and images of Blake continued to bombard her. Instead of the shower preparing her for a soothing slumber, it awakened urges that she wished she could get a handle on. Memories of Blake were alive. They taunted her.

Cadence sat up in bed and groaned. Racing thoughts chased her sleepiness away. Briefly, she entertained the idea of taking a sleeping pill, but it was too late for that. She'd never get up in time for work. Cadence reached over and grabbed the remote off the nightstand. The eleven o'clock news announced a second arrest and other new developments in the Banks scandal before going into a commercial break. Cadence flipped the channel. That was the last thing she needed to see or hear. At least she thought so until she saw the image of her ex, Kenny, on the screen standing between two women who looked as if they were about to claw one another's eyes out. Cadence sat up straighter and then leaned forward, squinting at the TV. Through narrowed vision, she recognized that one of the women was Kenny's new wife.

Pressing the info button on her remote, the description told her that she was watching their reality show, *The High Life*. This particular episode was about a face-off between Kenny's wife, Harper, and another woman regarding rumors of a bankruptcy. For a quick moment, Cadence thought about watching to see who was going bankrupt but thought better of how she wanted to spend her time. Evidently, the catfight ensued with Kenny right in the center, and Cadence laughed until her belly ached. If she needed more evidence to confirm that her ex was not the one for her, this was it. Unfortunately, those thoughts made her think about how Blake seemed to be so right—until now. Cadence continued flipping the channels but still couldn't find anything to hold her attention. She flopped back on the bed and laid there, swatting away thoughts of Blake until her eyes grew too heavy to stay open. Maybe she could sleep without Blake invading her dreams.

Cadence woke with a start. Her body lurched forward. She blinked rapidly and looked around the room. She shielded her eyes against the sliver of sun peeking through the window. It was seven minutes before her alarm was supposed to go off. Her hopes had failed her. Blake had not only invaded her dreams, he'd lit them on fire. Cadence continued panting as she sat up in bed trying to untangle reality from the illusory. She felt Blake's taut muscular body against hers. Her skin still burned from the electrifying kisses he had planted along her inner thighs. Both the perspiration that dotted her forehead and the flames ignited in her core existed without a doubt. She wiped her forehead and snatched the covers back. She was annoyed with herself for not being able to get him out of her system. She'd just have to work harder at pushing the effects of him aside, starting with a cool shower.

Chapter 27

By the time Cadence walked in, Blake was already set up in the conference room, flipping through papers with a cup of coffee in his hand. Blake's heart felt as if it could stop beating when he looked up and saw her. Immediately she averted her eyes. Chancing a quick peek, he looked her over and tried to contain his reaction to her presence. Seeing her face made him want to smile, but he kept his lips pressed together. Even if the circumstances weren't ideal, sharing the same space was far better than being on the other side of all his unanswered calls.

Cadence made it clear that involvement was all about business. Her clipped responses and the standoffish way she treated him showed that she was serious. Yet, under that hard professional exterior, he knew that she had to be just as affected by his presence as he was by hers. It took all of his energy and determination to keep from pulling her into his arms and kissing her. He'd give her the space she needed, but he wasn't going to give up on her—on them.

"Good morning." Cadence's greeting was short and void of any kind of cheer. She spread several folders across the table.

"Good morning to you." Blake muffled a chuckle. Her staunch effort to be aloof tickled him.

"What's so funny?"

She'd caught him. "Huh?" he asked, buying a few moments. "Oh. Nothing. You look tired."

"A little. I didn't get much sleep."

Several near-inappropriate innuendos teetered on the tip of his tongue. Blake knew better than to let them fly. "Up late...working?"

"Yes. On your case, of course." Cadence sat for the first time since entering the room. She groaned as she reached across the table for one of the files. "There's been a new arrest. The attorney general picked up Banks's former campaign manager yesterday."

"I know. They must have found something on him." Blake hung his head for a moment. "It's bad enough that they've got my face plastered across every network along with these men. I can't imagine being on camera while they're carrying me out in cuffs." Cadence tossed him a questionable look. "I didn't do anything." He responded to the accusations in her expression. "I've never been shy, but this is not the kind of attention a man craves."

"Last night I finished going through your company's files to ensure that there was nothing in your records that we needed to worry about."

"Didn't find anything, did you?" Blake was sure of himself.

"No."

"Told you."

"We still have to wait and see what's in the files that

Banks's attorneys are sending today. My hope is that they will come early. Once we go through those, I'd like to get the press conference scheduled, letting the media know that we are now representing you and we're confident that we will be able to show the public that you're innocent."

Blake sat all the way back in his chair. "I'll be glad when this is over."

"Me, too."

"Really?" Blake put his hand on his chest, pretending his feelings were hurt.

Cadence twisted her lips at him, dismissing his act.

Amy came bursting through the door with her jacket sliding off one shoulder and her purse still hanging from her arm. "So sorry I'm late. I'm going to drop my things off, grab the new intern and a cup of coffee, and I'll be right back."

As Amy shot back out of the office, Blake stood and made his way to Cadence's side of the table. He could tell by the way her shoulders hunched that she was uncomfortable with how close he came.

"I called you last night." Blake leaned against the sturdy table and crossed his arms.

"It was after hours." Cadence kept her eyes on the papers she was shuffling.

"I know, but now that I'm your client, do you think you can pick up my calls?"

"I'll answer any of your calls during working hours." Cadence straightened out the files in her hand, placed them back on the table and picked up a new pile.

"Do you think we will get a chance to talk?" Blake asked. Cadence still hadn't looked Blake's way.

"We've been talking for the past two days."

Blake's frustration wrangled with his emotions and both got the best of him. He snatched the file from Cadence's hand and tossed it on the table. The folder slid a few inches more after landing.

"Blake!" Cadence stood, meeting him eye to eye.

"This is the first time you've even looked me in the eye. This whole time, you've been treating me like a stranger that flattened your tires."

Cadence huffed. "This is neither the time nor the place for—"

"Then when and where?" he interjected. "You won't answer my calls outside of 'business hours.'" He curled his fingers into quotes and stared at her dead on.

"Besides this case, there's nothing for us to talk about." Cadence reached for the file that Blake had just confiscated from her.

"So that's it? Just like that?" Blake shook his head as his chest tightened. "We were building something special, Cadence. You can't tell me you didn't feel it, too."

Cadence didn't respond. She busied herself doing nothing in particular with all the documents scattered across the table. Then she got up and walked to the window, creating more distance between them.

Blake's shoulders drooped. He didn't mean to get upset, but he couldn't take much more of her coldness. He also didn't want this process to become rife with tension. He needed to be around her, even if he had to manage her cold shoulder. It was better than not being able to see her beautiful face. At least he was able to take in the sweet aroma of her perfume, despite the fact that her attitude toward him reeked. He would do what he could until things could be turned around.

Blake walked to where she stood facing New York City's West Side. "I'm sorry," he said, touching her shoulder. She flinched. "I didn't mean to get upset. It's just that this thing between us—"

Cadence spun toward him. "There's nothing between us, Mr. Barrington."

Blake removed his hand from her shoulder as if it burned his fingers. Her words cut him. The formal nature in which she spoke made them sound even colder. Rejection never swayed him. He was that confident. Yet Cadence's refutation punctured him. Now he questioned if continuing to pursue her would be worth it. Taking slow steps, he backed away, holding his hands up in surrender.

"My apologies, Ms. Payne." He felt his lips tighten as they normally did when he was irritated. He was done trying. Blake wasn't sure if he could say that he loved her, but it did feel as if she had reached into his chest, pulled his heart out, slayed it and put it back.

Just then, Amy returned with a slim, wide-eyed woman. It appeared as though she felt the tension in the room because she paused in the middle of announcing that she was back. "I…uh. I brought some more coffee." Cautiously, she and the intern placed the extra cups on the table.

"I'll get out of your way. Please be sure to notify me of any developments on my case." Begrudgingly, Blake made his way over to the chair he'd previously occupied, picked up his briefcase, copies of the documents and his coffee cup from earlier. "Amy. Thanks for the coffee, but I'm actually heading out." Blake forced a smile in Amy's direction and nodded politely at the other woman.

"Oh, Blake." She chuckled. "I mean, Mr. Barrington. Sorry."

"No, it's fine." Blake dismissed her apology.

"I'd like to introduce you to Katrina. She's one of our new interns. She'll be helping us out on the case."

Blake extended his hand to the young woman. "It's very nice to meet you."

Katrina tittered and with a coy smile she took Blake's

hand and managed a firm shake. "It's nice to meet you, too."

"Hmm. Great handshake!" Blake nodded his approval.

"Thank you, Mr. Barrington." Her demure grin returned.

Through his peripheral vision, Blake noticed Cadence's disapproving frown. He wasn't sure if her frown was meant for him or if it was because of the way Katrina gushed during their greeting. He hadn't missed that, either. Yet, he wasn't fazed. "Well, Amy," he said, turning his full attention toward her. "I'll assume that if you all need anything from me, I'll probably hear it from you."

"Most likely," Amy said optimistically, as if she was single-handedly trying to lift the thick cloud of tension that had settled in the room.

"Enjoy your day, ladies."

"You, too," Amy and Katrina said in unison.

Cadence gave no response.

As Blake walked out, he could hear Katrina whisper, "He's gorgeous." Amy shushed her.

When Blake reached the pavement in front of the building, he realized he still had the entire day ahead of him. His brother had taken over most of his cases, so he wasn't expected back at the office. He didn't want to go all the way back to Long Island, but he had to find something to distract himself from the way Cadence had him feeling.

Despite the few reporters still camped out at his office, he decided to go there to continue making notes in the case files. He wanted to be sure to explain anything that could come across as suspicious. At least that would give him something to do besides think about Cadence.

Hunter wasn't at the firm when Blake arrived. After greeting the others, Blake retreated to his office. The remainder of his morning was spent trying to focus and wondering how things had gotten so out of hand with

Cadence. He regretted getting emotional. She was right; her company's boardroom wasn't the time or the place to deal with his questions.

Blake didn't totally blame Cadence for her actions. They had only known each other a short time. She was just being cautious—and rightfully so. Against his true desire, he decided to give her the space she needed. If he could get them back to at least being friendly, he was sure she'd come around once she realized that he was completely innocent. In his mind, this made sense, although his heart wanted more.

Blake's phone buzzed and when he saw that the call was coming from Maco, Dunlop and Norman, he snatched it, swiped and answered.

"Mr. Barrington!" Amy's cheerful voice filled the line.

"Hey, Amy. How's it going?"

"Wonderful. I just wanted to let you know we've received the files from Banks's office. As soon as we get through those, Ms. Payne will be ready to schedule our press conference."

"Oh. Okay. Thanks."

"I'll call you if we need anything."

"Thanks again, Amy."

"You're welcome Mr. Barrington. Talk to you soon."

Blake put the phone down and rested his head in the palm of his hand. She could have easily texted him the same message. Something had to be done and Blake would have to be the one to initiate the action.

Chapter 28

It was another exhausting day. Cadence got home way after the rush hour crowd and again headed straight for the teakettle. This night, she hadn't brought home any work. She needed a mental break. Once the boxes of documents from Banks's office arrived, she, Katrina and Amy spent the afternoon going through what they could and then sitting in an endless meeting with Adam reporting all that they'd found in the case so far. She put the intern on researching briefs and outcomes of similar cases.

There was so much more to do, but all of that would have to wait until the next day. Tonight she planned to drink chamomile tea, soak in a bath and read a few chapters in one of the many books she started but never had the opportunity to finish. Then she would snuggle under the covers and watch TV until she fell asleep. She needed a break from the case and most of all from Blake.

Cadence shivered. Their little run-in earlier that day still pricked at her conscience. She tried to shake off the feeling that came over her. She hadn't meant to be mean to Blake, but she had to keep her distance. Her indifferent professional attitude was necessary. It took every ounce of restraint she had to keep from running after Blake when he stormed out of the boardroom. No one on the job knew that she and Blake had any kind of history and she intended to keep it that way.

Cadence dialed Alana to chat for a few minutes before settling down. She had missed a few of her calls and hadn't had a chance to call her back before now. If she didn't reach out to her best friend soon, she would be in for a real chastising.

"Well, hello, stranger!" Alana's animated voice blasted through the receiver.

"I know, I know. It's been so busy." Cadence filled the kettle with water and put it on the stove while she updated Alana on all the details about representing Blake—everything except for the part about her emotions twirling in such a fitful quandary every time he was around.

"I'm glad you're representing him. Now you'll see that he's innocent."

"You don't know that, Alana. It doesn't matter anyway. I still have to represent him."

"He'd never do such a thing. He's a stand-up guy, and besides, there are no women involved."

"What's that supposed to mean?" Cadence scrunched up her face as if Alana could see her through the phone.

"Because that's the only type of scandal a Barrington could be caught up in. Women have been known to fight over those brothers."

"Oh." Cadence didn't know if that was a good or bad thing. "Is that why you and Drew didn't work out?"

"Who said we didn't work out? Hey, this isn't about me. So, do the folks at the job know about you and Blake?"

Alana said, deflecting the conversation to Cadence and Blake.

"Of course not! There's nothing going on between us for them to know about."

"Cadence!" She could imagine Alana giving her the proverbial side-eye.

"What? There's nothing going on," Cadence repeated.

"Don't convict him without a trial."

"Whatever." Alana's comment hit a nerve. Cadence was merely afraid of being played. She even wished she had more control over her feelings for him.

"What did Blake say about this?"

"About what?"

"That fact that there's supposedly nothing going on between the two of you."

"What's there to say?"

"Uh-huh! You never had a discussion with him, did you?"

"Alana."

"Don't Alana me! Just don't let your scattered brain write a check that your heart is not willing to cash."

"What?" Cadence laughed. Alana was always remixing clichés.

"You know exactly what I mean."

"Listen, crazy! I have to run. This is the first night this week that I got home at a decent time and there's a warm bath full of bubbles calling my name. I'll chat with you later. Okay?" she said as she poured the steaming water from the teakettle into her favorite mug.

"Okay, but remember what I said."

"Bye, girl!" Cadence ended the call, still chuckling.

After Cadence's bath was drawn, she picked up her mug and one of her unfinished legal thrillers, and stepped into the tub. She swore she could feel the tension fall away as the warm fragrant water enveloped her. Cadence laid her head back against her bath pillow to rest her eyes for a few moments.

When she popped her eyes open, she felt disoriented. She had obviously fallen asleep and had no idea how long. Her skin had pruned. The hot water was now lukewarm. The bubbles had dissipated and her tea was cold. She had never even cracked the book open.

At least her sleep was peaceful. Blake hadn't even stolen into her dreams as he had all those other times. Cadence washed up and then slipped into a comfortable cotton nightie. She padded down the carpeted steps to the kitchen so she could refresh her cup of tea, when she heard the doorbell.

Cadence looked over at the digital time display on the microwave. It was almost ten at night. She tipped to the window near the door to peek out. She wasn't expecting anyone and it couldn't have been her father. He always called before coming so he wouldn't waste a trip. Cadence looked out the window and her heart felt as if it would leap through her chest.

Letting the curtain fall back into place, Cadence took a deep breath, closed her eyes and exhaled slowly before pulling the door open. Blake stood before her as tall, handsome and gorgeous as ever. When his eyes took a slow journey down to her bare legs and back up to her face, she was reminded that the only thing between Blake's eyes and her skin was the short nightie. Cadence stepped back and pushed the door in front of her, peering around the edge at Blake.

"What are you doing here?"

"Can I come in?"

Cadence looked down at her bare feet and thought for a moment. She wanted to let him. Her heart was doing somersaults inside her chest. "Blake. I don't think this is a good idea."

"I'll only be a minute. I want to apologize for my behavior earlier, and since you never answer my calls outside of 'office hours,' I figured I had to drop by in order to do it face-to-face."

With an overt sigh, Cadence shook her head and said, "Okay." Before Blake could lift his foot to step in the door, Cadence added, "Just give me a minute." She closed the door on him.

She rushed up to her room and grabbed the first robe she could put her hands on and headed back downstairs. The one she picked was long, silky and silver. Sliding her arms through the cool soft fabric, she thought about a more casual alternative, perhaps her cotton one or the fluffy number she snuggled into during the winter months. She didn't want to give Blake the wrong idea. Most important, she needed to cover her nipples, which poked against her nightgown, and reduce the chances of Blake getting an eyeful when she sat since she didn't have on panties.

Cadence wrapped herself in the robe and pulled the belt tight. After another breath, she opened the door. Blake was leaning against the railing. Cadence swallowed hard after glancing at how well his jeans fit his frame. She cleared her throat, capturing his attention.

"You can come in now."

Blake raised his brows at her robe. "Again, I'm sorry for dropping in on you like this."

Cadence didn't respond. She closed the door and headed toward the kitchen.

"I was just making tea. Would you like some?"

Blake chuckled. "Got anything stronger?"

Cadence moved toward her cabinet.

"No! I was just kidding."

"Oh," she said. "Well, please have a seat." She swept her hand toward the kitchen table.

"I wish you would stop being so formal with me."

Cadence tilted her head but didn't respond. She needed to keep things professional. If not, she couldn't be held responsible for her impulses. Blake looked absolutely scrumptious in that button-down that fit snugly enough over his taut pecs. It was hard enough to be as cordial as she was.

Cadence was a thinker. She made safe decisions—ones that didn't result in jeopardizing consequences. Caution and reason were vital apparatuses in her decision-making tool kit. She almost never acted on impulse, despite the fact that she admired those who sometimes did. However, Blake Barrington had a way of getting her to dismiss her normal sensibilities.

"Cadence, please accept my apology for the way I acted earlier today. You were right. It was not the right time or place. It's just that I can't get used to this side of you. It felt so—" Blake paused as if he was searching the atmosphere for the right word "—cold. It was so unlike the woman I had the pleasure of getting to know." Cadence looked down into her teacup. "I didn't mean to upset you. I know this is a lot to take in right now. On one hand we know each other very well…" Blake paused, letting that sink in. "And, on the other hand, I guess we *don't* know each other all that well. Just in case you still have doubts, I'm innocent, but you'll realize that soon enough. I think it's important for us to at least be friendly until this is all over with."

"I apologize, too. I've been under a lot of pressure at work, so I could have been taking that out on you, too."

"No problem."

For a few moments, they sat in awkward silence. Cadence wasn't sure whether to initiate his exit or just keep cool. After his apology, she didn't want to come across as rude.

"Would you like some bottled water for the road?"

Blake stood. "I guess that's my cue."

"I'm sorry. I didn't mean—"

"It's no problem. I should be going." Despite Blake's words, he hadn't moved toward the door. His eyes locked in on her.

Cadence's heart beat slightly faster under his observation. She looked down to make sure her robe hadn't loosened. Finally, she stood and started toward the door. She caught the scent of Blake's cologne as she passed by. He followed closely behind and a nervous energy churned in her stomach. Her body betrayed her practical mind. Desire began a slow build inside her. Blake was too close. She pepped up her step, creating more space between them. By the time she reached the front door, her heart was pounding. She swore if Blake got close enough he would hear it.

She reached for the door handle and before she could turn it, Blake's hand covered hers. His body pressed against her back.

"I miss you," he whispered in her ear from behind. She could feel the heat of his breath on her back.

Cadence swallowed and opened her mouth, but only a slight gasp came out. A flash of heat shot through her. She stood there willing her mind to take charge because her desire had already won her body over. The place between her thighs grew warm. She was quickly losing the battle against caution and reason and anything else that told her to just open the door and make him leave.

Blake pushed up against her, closing out any possible space between them. Cadence felt his strong chest and swelling erection against her back. She whimpered after trying a weak attempt to get her bearings together.

"Did you hear me?" Blake's husky, breathy inquiry blazed a trail of heat across the back of her neck. "I've missed you so much."

Cadence closed her eyes. She'd missed him, too. Her

recent intimate interactions with him were spent only in her dreams. Now he was here—in the flesh. The passion she felt right now was real, evident in the moisture building in her center.

Blake nuzzled his nose in her hair. He took in her scent and moaned. "You smell so good. Don't you miss me, Cadence?"

The sultry way he called her name made her want to scream. She kept her mouth clamped shut, afraid of what sound might escape. Her knees threatened to crumble beneath her. In the limited space between them, Cadence turned around, feeling every part of his muscular torso in the process, leaving a raging hot path along her skin. Before she could open her mouth to protest, Blake covered her mouth with his, kissing her until she felt like a feather floating through the air on a sunny day. Leaving her breathless, he gave her a quick break before capturing her mouth again.

Interlocking his fingers with hers, Blake held them as his passion poured out through his kisses. When he released her lips the second time, both of them gasped. Allowing her to catch her breath, Blake continued his zealous assail across her throat and down her neck.

Suddenly he stopped. Cadence's eyes popped open. She hadn't realized they were closed until then. She looked up to find Blake staring down at her.

"I'm sorry." The sincere look in Blake's eyes made her heart swell. "I shouldn't have done that. If you want me to stop, I will."

Cadence didn't want him to stop. She found herself licking the remnants of his taste from her lips. Her expression pleaded with him. Taking that for his answer, Blake loosened the belt on her robe and rubbed his thumbs across her hardening nipples through her nightgown. Cadence's eyes closed involuntarily and a moan rose in her throat.

Blake covered her mouth again, siphoning the moan out of her. Their hands roamed one another desperately as if they were trying to find their way to each other through the dark.

Blake lifted her into his arms. Cadence wrapped her legs around him. Their lips never parted as he carried her up the stairs and into her bedroom.

Gently Blake laid her on the bed and removed her robe and nightie. He caressed her skin, reacquainting himself with her territory. His touch sparked new firestorms. Slowly he stood, removed his clothes and slipped on a condom before joining her again.

Cadence couldn't stand it any longer. Suddenly she was in a rush to feel him. She pulled him over her and guided him inside. When they connected, stars exploded, causing flecks of passion to burst all over her. The room was filled with the sounds of their delight. Their bodies slapped as they called on each other. His grunts grew into a growl and her whimpers morphed into screams at the pinnacle of the most exhilarating release Cadence had ever experienced. It took several moments for them to return to real time and space.

Blake held her as if letting her go would make her cease to exist. His penetrating embrace filled up every void. Cadence would worry about tomorrow when it came. Right now, she savored the bliss of his powerful arms and the delicious joy she felt from giving in to her impulses.

Chapter 29

Despite lack of sleep, Blake woke with a sated smile. He and Cadence couldn't seem to get enough of one another the night before. They continued to make love well into the early morning. Blake got home with just enough time for a few additional winks before having to get ready for the day. Tired but still energetic, Blake hummed through this morning routine.

Regardless of his bad fortune with the Banks's scandal, he couldn't remember feeling better. Cadence had finally let him back into her world. As he dressed for the day, he promised himself that he would keep his senses in her presence. The last thing he wanted to do was lose ground with her.

Blake texted a simple Good morning and was relieved that she had responded adding a smiley emoticon. His grin spread across his face and remained there until he walked out of the house. He didn't believe the effect this woman had on him and couldn't recall a time when any woman ruled his mind and emotions the way Cadence did. The playboy was in jeopardy of losing his VIP status.

By the time Blake worked his way through the rush-hour crowd and then through the few reporters still camped out in front of his building, he had begun to feel the effects of his lack of sleep from the previous night. He already had several messages on both his cell and office phones. Quickly, he'd gone through them, hoping to hear something promising about the state of the case. There were still no messages from Banks or his team. Blake swallowed his disappointment. He knew Banks was probably still in jail, but he had hoped to hear from members of his team, whom he had called to investigate how he'd been tossed into this whole thing.

The recent arrest of Banks's accountant unnerved him, as well. On one hand, Blake knew that the attorney general wouldn't pick up anyone unless he was sure he had something solid on the person. Yet, Blake was smart enough to know that the system didn't always operate by the letter. Cases like this, people were often made examples of because the public was hungry for a resolution. He'd already witnessed more slighted social media and blog posts from a few self-appointed political critics. One of the late-night talk-show hosts had even made fun of the situation in his opening monologue. Fortunately for Blake, most of the fingers were pointed at Banks, not the others mentioned in the scandal. Blake just hoped that this nightmare would be over soon. When Blake's cell phone rang and Cadence's number flashed across the screen, he couldn't help smiling.

"You need to get here now." Cadence's voice filled the line with an urgency that made Blake's smile fall and his pulse quicken.

"What's going on?" Blake stood, no longer able to sit still.

"Just get here ASAP," Cadence snapped and ended the call.

Blake flew past Hunter's open office door. By the time he reached the elevator bank, Hunter was on his heels.

"What's the matter? Where's the fire?"

"Cadence called. She said to get to her office right away. She must have found something, but it sure doesn't sound good."

"I'm coming with you. "

As much as Blake would have loved his brother's support, he needed to face Cadence alone—especially after the night they'd had. "Don't worry. I have it. I'll call you as soon as I know what's up."

Hunter hesitated, looking as though he wasn't willing to take no for an answer. After another moment, he dropped his shoulder and said, "Okay, but I'll be waiting for your call."

"When I know something, you'll know something." The elevator doors opened and Blake stepped on. Once they shut, he took a deep breath and held it for a moment, hoping to slow his heart rate.

Nothing seemed to happen fast enough for Blake. He stood for several minutes trying to hail a cab. When he finally got one, the driver crept along as though he was driving Miss Daisy instead of New York City's infamous taxi. The lobby of Cadence's building was flooded with professionals and delivery personnel carrying or going out for lunch. The elevator filled up twice before he could get in. However, once he arrived on Cadence's floor, he was immediately whisked into the conference room where Cadence, Adam, Seth, Amy and the intern all moved about the large table, frantically sifting through papers and chatting on cell phones.

Blake's heart felt as if it had sunk deeper into his chest. For several moments, no one had even noticed that he was there. Blake cleared his throat. "Counselor Payne?" he addressed Cadence.

"Mr. Barrington," Adam responded. "Please have a seat." Adam redirected his focus. "Amy, please bring that laptop over here and set it in front of Mr. Barrington."

"Yes, sir." Amy scurried to the opposite end of the table to retrieve the laptop.

"Can someone explain to me what's going on?" Blake asked. Cadence shot him a look he couldn't decipher. Was she mad, disappointed? He couldn't tell.

This time, Adam cleared his throat. "We've noticed a few inconsistencies when we compared payments that went out from Banks's accounts to yours. They don't show up in your company records, but on Banks's side we can see that these checks have been cleared."

Blake's eyes widened and he lifted slightly from the chair. "What? Are you imply—"

"We are not implying anything, Blake." Adam's tone was warmer as he pat Blake's back. "We just need to make sure that we uncover any and every possible item that the attorney general could try to use against us."

"I gave you everything." Blake was getting upset. Cadence hadn't said one word to him since he entered the room. She in all of her beautiful splendor, arms crossed, eyeing him suspiciously. Adam was doing all the talking, which was unusual since he hardly ever made their meetings.

"I know you did, Blake, but we have to be completely thorough. The AG hasn't come against you yet. I believe it's because they haven't found anything sufficient enough to come after you with, but we need to be ready in case they try. Now, I need to understand what's happening with the missing checks that were made out to you before anyone else comes knocking on our door asking the same question."

"I told you, I'm innocent." Blake felt as if he was losing his cool. "I didn't hide anything." Blake spoke to Adam but looked at Cadence. She turned away and Blake thought his heart stopped beating for a quick second. He couldn't handle the idea that she thought of him as anything but an honorable man. His integrity was at stake with her and that bothered him more than having his reputation publicly destroyed. He wasn't falling for the public. He was falling for Cadence.

"I don't doubt that you're innocent," Adam said with firm confidence. That gave Blake some comfort. Cadence's chilly demeanor still bothered him. "You use online banking, I assume."

Blake furrowed his brows. "Yes, but…why? I don't follow."

"We need to take a look at your personal financials."

Blake closed his eyes and took a moment to collect himself. He understood Adam's request. Blake had asked clients for more personal information than this. Blake looked up at Adam standing over his shoulder. Adam returned a reassuring nod.

Blake turned to the laptop and began to pull up his banking information. Since it was an unrecognized computer that he was using, first he had to get an authorization code emailed to him. Blake retrieved the numbers from his email and after a few clicks of the keyboard, information from two different accounts appeared on the screen.

"We'll need to print your statements from the last five years," Adam added.

"Five years!" Blake lifted from his seat.

"I'm afraid so, but don't worry. We will ensure that your account credentials will remain confidential. This is something we take very seriously here at our firm."

Shaking his head, Blake sat back down and began pulling up statements to be printed. More than an hour had passed before Blake reached the end of the statements. The paper in the printer had to be replenished several times. Every member of his legal team seemed to be engrossed in a specific task. Adam had left the room, returning periodically to check in. Seth had at least made an attempt to make reassuring small talk with Blake a few times as he asked for clarification on some documents Blake previously provided. Amy and the intern made a run for coffee, juice and tea. Cadence continued to keep her distance.

Upon Amy's return, she sent the intern to fetch the printout of Blake's bank statements. Then she and Seth eagle-eyed Blake's accounts for any debits or credits that would appear suspicious. They came to Blake with anything they found questionable.

Fortunately for Blake, he was able to identify every credit or debit that linked him to the congressman, which included ticket purchases for fund-raising dinners during Banks's campaign. Banks had also paid Blake on several occasions to speak at fund-raising events for Billy's Promise, making those checks out to Blake directly.

Adam returned to the conference room and the team provided a full report of their findings. When the muscles in Adam's face softened, showing his relief, Blake felt as if he could breathe again. The room seemed lighter. He appeared to be reassured that the trek through Blake's personal financials didn't reveal anything they couldn't explain.

"One more thing, Blake," Adam said, commanding everyone's attention. "You do know that we have to turn over these finding to the attorney general if they ask?"

"I realize that. No problem."

"Thanks for tending to this so promptly. Our next step is to get a response out to the public. They've been waiting to hear from our side." Adam looked at his watch. "How about we call it a day and get something drafted for the media first thing in the morning?"

"That sounds like a plan," Seth said, straightening the papers in front of him.

"Let's put all of this in my office until tomorrow," Cadence said. "We all need a good night's sleep so we can be camera ready. Once we let folks know that we will be releasing a statement, the media will come running in abundance," she added. That was the first statement that Cadence had made to Blake since he'd arrived, although it was only remotely directed his way.

Blake's gaze locked in on her as he reached for his briefcase. He waited for her to look his way. When their eyes met, he refused to turn away, knowing the intensity of his gaze seemed to make her uncomfortable. He didn't care. He needed her to acknowledge him. A beat later, she turned away. After such a magical night, he never imagined that the next time he saw her it would be under such duress.

Blake hung back as each of them filed out of the conference room. His eyes were still on Cadence.

"Counselor Payne?" he beckoned as she was about to pass, touching her arm. Amy and the intern walked around her.

Cadence paused but didn't turn in his direction.

"Can we speak in private?"

Cadence blinked a few times. "Sure," she said, mustering up a feigned cheer in her tone. "Amy, I'll meet you guys in my office." When the others were out of earshot, Cadence continued, "What can I do for you, Blake?" Her body had relaxed slightly. Her tone wasn't as cold.

"I'm innocent."

"I know that, Blake."

"So what happened here today?"

"I was just doing my job. That's what you pay me for." Cadence avoided Blake's pleading eyes.

"Last night—"

"Was a mistake." Cadence interjected, completing the sentence for him. "We should have never let it happen. I'm sorry, Blake." She walked off, leaving Blake behind to mull over her statement.

Unfamiliar with the notion of being at a loss for words, Blake stood blinking at her response. His lungs felt as if someone had pumped them with too much air.

Chapter 30

For the past week and a half, Cadence kept her distance from Blake, channeling most of their required communication through Amy. She also had Amy tell him that it wasn't necessary to come to the office while they waited to hear from the attorney general.

Sleeping with him had been risky. Once again, her sensibilities had taken leave. Cadence remembered the look on his face that day in the conference room when she told him that it was a mistake. He seemed to be genuinely offended. With the case coming to a close, she wondered if she'd ever see him again. They could remain friends, but would he be willing?

"Ugh!" Cadence groaned, and stepped into the office with her shoulders slumped. Blake had managed to leave an imprint on her heart. He challenged her, made her laugh from deep down inside and compelled her body to do things she never thought she'd do. With him, she was spontaneous—adventurous, even, and she loved that. To top it off, he was good-looking, caring and smart.

"Are you okay?" Amy asked with her face scrunched as Cadence walked by.

"Huh. Oh. I'm fine," Cadence said. Amy followed her into the office. "I just need a minute," she said.

"No problem. I'll run get us some coffee." Amy headed back through the door. "The usual?" she turned back and asked just before making her exit.

"Yes. Oh, wait. Get me half of that one with the extra energy boost and half hazelnut, please." Amy disappeared and Cadence melted into her office chair, propped her elbows on her desk, held her palms to her forehead and sighed. She couldn't let this get in the way of work, but she couldn't get over the fact that she would no longer have a reason to see Blake after this and wondered if they should go their separate ways.

Cadence retrieved her cell phone from her purse and dialed his number. The call went to voice mail so she hung up. At this point, leaving him a voice mail or text wouldn't suffice. She needed to speak with him in person.

Amy knocked and pushed the door open. Cadence put her phone down and looked up. "What's up?"

"Just letting you know that I'm not going down to get coffee anymore. There's breakfast set up in the conference room for the entire office. They want us all in there at ten o'clock sharp."

Cadence looked at her watch. She had forty-five minutes to go. "Okay. I can wait."

The second Amy closed the door, Cadence's mind went right back to Blake and his case. Adam had invested more time in working the case in the past few weeks. Working around the clock, they'd presented the attorney general with their argument to avoid an indictment against Blake. Awaiting their decision was grueling. Finally, they announced that Blake and two others were no longer considered persons of interest.

Banks, his campaign manager and accountant were the real culprits and had been charged with several counts of fraud for misappropriating funds for both the organization and his last political campaign. The accountant blew the case open when he cut a deal that exposed all of Banks's criminal activities as well as a few other high-profile clients who had him cooking their books. This development sparked new media frenzy once the attorney general started handing out indictments like candy on Halloween. And it had all started with a disgruntled employee who had been fired by Banks's office a few weeks before.

Banks was forced to resign from his position as a congressman, as well as executive director of the organization. On top of that, he had to pay more than $1.5 million in restitution.

Blake was asked to replace Banks as the executive director of Billy's Promise but declined the offer. Most recently, he was reinstated as a board member of the NYAA.

Cadence looked at the time on her cell phone. Thirty minutes had passed. It was time to head upstairs for that meeting Amy mentioned. When she arrived, Adam, Seth, Kerry, Amy and other coworkers were sipping on cups of coffee and munching on pastries. Blake walked in and she stiffened for a moment before easing her lips into a coy smile.

Adam welcomed him with a firm shake. "Congratulations once again."

"I have you all to thank for this. I appreciate the time and energy you put in to helping me save my reputation." Blake paused slightly as his eyes landed on Cadence. "You believed in me." She averted her eyes. "And I want to thank you for giving me your all. I finally have my life back. I've imagined what it would be like to be famous and this wasn't it." His last response generated chuckles around the room.

Adam nodded with a proud smile. "You were an ideal client."

"Thanks." Blake pulled an envelope containing the final payment from his briefcase. "And this is for you." Adam took the check and nodded once again before handing it over to his secretary.

"Everyone, please have a cup of coffee and something to eat. We have a few announcements to share. Mr. Barrington, you are welcome to join us. No need to rush off. You may be interested in hearing one of our announcements."

"I'll just grab a cup of coffee, if you don't mind."

"Sure," Adam replied.

As people crowded the credenzas, picking from an aromatic selection of muffins, pastries and beverages, Blake walked a direct line to where Cadence stood. She felt him coming.

"Good morning," he said to her back.

She turned slowly. "Good morning to you and congratulations once again."

"I want to personally thank you. I know you felt blind-sided by this, but you worked hard and I appreciate that."

"Oh…you're welcome," Cadence said as if she was surprised by his sentiment. "Um… I'd like to talk with you later. Will you have time after work?"

Blake paused for a moment. "Sure."

"Nothing big or alarming, I just want to clear up a few things," she said, dismissing any sense of urgency.

"Where would you like to meet?"

"How about Timothy's Coffeehouse over on Seventh?"

Adam cleared his throat, snagging the attention of everyone in the room. Blake nodded at Cadence and both turned in Adam's direction.

"Ladies and gentlemen... I hope you've all had a chance to grab something to eat. I'd like to begin." Around the room, people nodded their agreement. "Great." Adam continued, "First, I would like to recognize the team that worked on Mr. Barrington's case. You all did a splendid job. Kudos to each of you. You've made Maco, Dunlop and Norman look good." Adam nodded at each team member.

Staffers clapped their hands and a few even hooted, except Kerry.

"Who is that?" Blake leaned over and whispered in Cadence's ear. Amy obviously heard him because she snickered.

"Oh. That's my nemesis, Kerry Cooper," Cadence leaned in and whispered back.

"She doesn't look very happy."

"She's never happy when I receive accolades."

"Oh," Blake said.

Adam continued, "I'd also like to take this opportunity to announce that our illustrious partner, Scott Hagen, will be leaving the firm." Ohs and gasps rang out throughout the room. Scott, an older partner with a distinguished blend of salt-and-pepper hair nodded, acknowledging the group's sentiment.

"Scott will be relocating to Florida and has begun the process of opening his very own firm there. Hagen and Associates!" Adam raised his coffee cup in a toast-like manner and the room exploded in applause.

"We'll miss you, Scott!" an associate called out, starting a rise in similar sentiments.

Tapping his coffee cup with a pen, Adam brought the room back into order. "That brings us to our last announcement for the morning. "With Scott's departure, which will be effective this week—" a few more gasps erupted "—we have decided to fill his position immediately so that he may begin transitioning his caseload to the new partner."

A slow, confident smile spread across Kerry's face and she balled her hands into hopeful fists.

"Ladies and gentlemen, I present to you our newest partner…" Adam stopped speaking as wonder and suspense filled in the space of his dramatic pause. Kerry's smile grew wider and she self-assuredly stepped forward. "Cadence Payne!"

Kerry's loud gasp took all of the attention away from Cadence. Everyone looked at her. Quickly, she shut her mouth and looked downward before attempting a full recovery. "Cadence!" she said with feigned glee. Instead, her cheeks burned with embarrassment and she walked toward Cadence as if her legs would give out at any moment. "Congratulations!" Kerry extended her hand to Cadence and gripped her in a stiff handshake and then walked straight out of the boardroom.

Cadence's colleagues took turns congratulating both her and Scott with more handshakes, hugs and kind words.

Blake stood aside giving her space as she beamed with pride. Minutes after, everyone began clearing the conference room. Cadence had been summoned by Adam to stop by his office.

"I guess I'll see you later, Blake. Thanks for agreeing to meet with me," Cadence said.

"Wait!" Blake caught her arm as she turned to leave. "Congratulations." He looked into her eyes with such intensity that Cadence could hardly stand it.

She didn't answer but hung back as everyone else exited the conference room.

Adam nodded at her and winked at Blake. Cadence wondered how much Adam had discerned in the past few weeks. They had to be fools to think that no one could suspect that they knew each other well before the case.

Blake smiled back at Adam and then waved. "It's been a pleasure, Adam."

"Yes, it has," Adam replied and left.

When the room was empty except for Cadence and Blake, she busied herself by fidgeting. She looked everywhere except at him.

"Like I was saying, I want to congratulate you on your promotion." He gently held her hands, leaned in and kissed her. At first she didn't oblige, but then quickly gave in to the magical feel of his plump lips. Cadence opened her mouth and kissed him back. Every emotion she'd been holding back was unleashed as he held her in his arms. Blake kissed her so hungrily that she had to pull away to breathe.

Cadence covered her mouth with her hand and looked away, embarrassed for displaying such abandonment. She'd almost forgotten that she was at work.

"I've wanted to do that for weeks. Will you let me do it again?"

Cadence licked her lips, and after a moment of pondering, Blake pulled her in tighter and kissed her as if it were the last time he'd ever be able to taste her delicious lips. When he released her, she gasped.

Holding her chin up, Blake searched her eyes. "I don't want to be friends with you," he said.

"I don't want to be friends with you, either," Cadence replied.

This time she pulled him in for the kiss and just as their waiting lips were about to connect, someone cleared their throat. They jerked away from one another, avoiding eye contact. Cadence held her head down and smiled at her own embarrassment.

"I'm sorry to interrupt. I just came back to clean up," Adam's secretary said as she stepped into the room.

"No problem," Cadence said, fidgeting with her hands.

Blake's smile was full of mischief.

"You know what? I'll just come back."

The second she left the room, Blake and Cadence burst out laughing.

Chapter 31

Blake connected his Bluetooth speaker to his iPad, tapped the Pandora app and tuned in to the R&B/soul radio station. Joe's sultry voice slipped in like silk, crisp and clear, as if he were standing in Blake's living room singing in the flesh. The meal Blake prepared filled his entire first floor with savory scents. Soft lighting illuminated each room and fragrant candles flickered at the dining table. Instead of the friendly chat at the local coffeehouse that Cadence suggested, Blake persuaded her to let him make her a celebratory meal. He wanted to pump his fists when she said yes.

Blake sent one more text to the driver to make sure that he had arrived at Cadence's house on time. He wished he could have been there to see the surprised look on her face when she realized that he'd sent a limo for her. He determined that his time would be better spent preparing an appetizing meal and creating the right atmosphere for their evening together. The driver texted back, telling Blake that Ms. Payne was in the car and they were on their way.

Blake raced around his house, preparing for the evening. He smiled every time he thought about their kiss at her office. Remembering her reaction, Blake's confidence kicked in. He had gotten Cadence back in his arms and wasn't wasting any time guiding their relationship to the next level. Thoughts about Cadence caused his heart, mind and other parts to respond as he remembered her soft lips against his.

Checking his reflection, Blake was pleased with his decision to wear black slacks and a V-neck sweater that showed undeniable evidence of his workout regimen. Blake fingered his goatee and nodded before turning to assess the atmosphere. Again, he surmised that everything was just right.

Blake heard the two quick taps on the car's horn, indicating the limousine's arrival, and met them at the door. When Cadence stepped in, he held her by both hands and licked his lips as his eyes cascaded over her from top to bottom. "Damn!" Blake ran his fingers through her loose hair and admired the single-shouldered shirt, wet-looking leggings and high-heeled boots Cadence donned. She had let her hair down. Soft curls bounced against her shoulders. "You are beautiful." Before she could respond, he wrapped his arms around her waist and captured her lips, letting his tongue go on a sweet expedition.

"Will that be all, sir?" the driver asked from behind Cadence.

Blake nodded without breaking his kiss and then heard the front door close. They remained there, hands searching each other's bodies, becoming reacquainted. Blake blazed a trail of hot kisses along her bare shoulder.

Words failed to describe how Cadence made him feel. Blake held her tighter, pulling her in even closer. "I'm glad you're here." He laid his forehead against hers.

"Me, too," Cadence said. They held on to one another

for a while. Finally, Cadence spoke, slicing through the contented silence. "We should probably eat. I'm pretty hungry."

The two laughed and Blake took her by the hand and led her to the dining room. Place settings were positioned at each end of the table, with candles in the center. Rounding Cadence, Blake pulled out her chair, waited for her to sit and then disappeared into the kitchen to make their plates.

Instead of sitting on the opposite side, he abandoned his usual place setting and sat right next to her. They laughed and flirted until their meal was done. Then they nibbled on each other, sipping champagne until desire chided him to take things a little further. To his surprise and delight, Cadence rose from her seat, stood over him and slowly lowered herself onto his lap. A cool smile slid across his face. He loved having her take the lead. His erection grew stiff against her and she held her pelvis against him.

Blake nestled his nose in the crook of her neck and ran his fingers through her hair. Holding her firmly, he lifted up and laid her on the table. Locking his hands with hers, he leaned over and kissed her some more. Cadence lifted slightly, and Blake followed her lead, giving her space to stand. Cadence took him by the hand and led him down the hall to his bedroom. Relieving him of his clothes, piece by piece, she stripped him down until he sported nothing but a rigid erection. She massaged it to a new level of firmness. Blake's head lolled back and he moaned.

He returned the favor by helping her out of her clothes, one garment at a time. Cadence sat back on the bed as Blake crawled toward her with desire so unbridled it felt as if he could spontaneously combust. He wanted her so badly the need nearly blinded him.

Blake burrowed his head between her thighs and then nibbled and sucked until he drove Cadence to a climax that shifted her back in a hard arch and caused her muscles to clench repeatedly. Cadence turned him over and took him into her mouth until he pulled himself away. Blake stared intently into her eyes. When he entered her, his eyes rolled shut. His head juddered back. Cadence cried out. Together they moved in harmony until their bodies shook as forceful releases ripped through them, leaving them hopelessly breathless and deliciously spent.

They lay cuddled as they caught their breath.

"So I can finally chuck that friend card you tried to hand me?" Blake broke the tranquil silence.

"Yeah." Cadence giggled. "Friends don't really act like this, do they?"

"No. They. Don't. Or. At. Least. They. Shouldn't." Blake kissed her between each word. "But people in relationships do."

"Oh. So we're in a relationship?" Cadence teased.

"We're practically on our way down the aisle." Blake tossed her an incredulous gaze.

Cadence gasped and then giggled. "Blake!" she said in a chiding manner.

"Oh. You didn't know?" he said, maintaining a dubious stare.

Cadence stared at him with her jaw hanging.

Casting the playfulness aside, Blake's countenance became serious. "I knew from the first day I saw you that there was something special about you. When you distanced yourself from me, that's when I knew I didn't want to live without you."

"Really?"

"Yeah, but I had to be patient. You were worth waiting for. I knew you would come around. You wanted me." Blake smirked, returning to his spirited quirkiness.

Cadence slapped Blake's shoulder and then threw her arms around his neck. Pulling back yet remaining in his arms, she searched his eyes. "I'm so sorry, Blake. I shouldn't have doubted you." She drew in a deep breath and exhaled slowly before asking, "Will you forgive me?"

"Only if you think you could marry a man like me."

Cadence's mouth dropped open again. She recovered with a faraway pensive gleam in her eyes. After a moment, she nodded. "Yes! I could marry a man like you!"

"Good, because I don't plan on letting you get away from me again." Blake's body responded with the same level of enthusiasm as his heart. He pressed his firmness against her, ready for round two.

Chapter 32

Several months later

As the day dipped into the horizon on an unusually balmy fall evening, Cadence found herself standing near the pier in Chelsea. This spot, just a few blocks from her new West Side office, had become a familiar place for her to clear her mind. She found the view and sounds of the Hudson and the droning of the cars jetting along the highway quite soothing. Right now, Cadence needed a moment.

Her newest client, a mistress who was allegedly raped by her lover's business partner, had been the topic of breaking news reports for the past few weeks. The famed Wall Street firm and renowned founders had landed themselves in the center of the latest media frenzy. Cadence and Alana's new firm, Payne and Tate LLC, had quickly developed a penchant for attracting high-profile cases in the short time since they'd opened.

Cadence looked up and smiled when she finally saw Blake heading her way with bags in his hands.

Blake wrapped his arms around her and planted several quick kisses on her lips, bringing her mind back to the present. "Crazy week, huh?"

"Yeah. The media will do anything for an 'exclusive' nugget." Cadence shook her head. "And then Alana cut out on me right after lunch. She said she had some family thing to take care of but wouldn't offer up any details. I hope everything is okay. She doesn't usually keep stuff from me."

Blake shook his head, took Cadence by the hand and started walking back toward her office. "Well, I've got something to help take your mind off all of that." He held up the bags.

Cadence stopped walking. "What are you up to, Blake?"

Blake turned around and grabbed her hand again. "Come on. Don't be scared."

"Ugh! It scares me whenever you tell me not to be scared."

"Don't worry. I think you'll enjoy this."

Then Cadence noticed that Blake was dressed rather nicely in a cool tan suit. "You look snazzy, babe." She looked down at his other hand. "Now, tell me what's in the bag."

"Stop asking so many questions and just follow my lead!"

Cadence chuckled. "The last time you told me that, I ended up Jet Skiing across Long Island Sound. I don't feel like jumping out of any airplanes, Blake."

He laughed. "Nothing like that—this time." He winked.

Blake led her back to her building. Inside, all of her employees had gone home. In her office, he shut the door, and after kissing her with an intensity that she could never get tired of, he stepped back and handed her the bags he'd been holding.

Smiling, Cadence pulled out a beautiful jade green cocktail dress and a pair of silver pumps.

"Where are we going?"

Blake put his finger to her lips. She giggled against them and nibbled one playfully.

Blake released her so she could go to the bathroom and freshen up her mascara and gloss. He put the extra bags on the side of her desk before leaving. Back on the street, he hailed a taxi. Cadence strained to hear the destination but couldn't make out what Blake had said. The suspense made her giddy.

"Okay. If you won't tell me where we're going, then can you tell me what inspired this little surprise?"

Blake dropped his jaw. "You don't know what today is?"

Cadence became alarmed. She jogged her mind into action. Did she forget something? Cadence was a stickler at keeping a schedule. She pulled out her cell phone and checked her calendar. As far as she knew, she hadn't missed anything.

When she looked up, Blake was still staring at her, waiting for a response.

"Did I miss something?" She gave voice to the question in her mind.

Blake shook his head, placing a hand on his heart. "I can't believe you don't remember."

Cadence was about to feel bad until she noticed Blake's slick smile. She poked his shoulder. "Don't do that."

Blake laughed. "You'll find out soon enough."

Cadence settled into the crook of his arm and a short while later, they arrived at the West Side Heliport.

"We're going on a helicopter ride? Oh my goodness!" Cadence clapped her hands, barely able to contain her excitement. Blake had awakened her predilection for adventure in the time they'd been together.

"Yes, but the night won't stop here."

Blake was right. The helicopter ride was just the beginning. Cadence sat staring out the window in childlike wonder, and the aircraft cruised along the Hudson while the pilot pointed out famous New York City and New Jersey landmarks. Soon after, they landed alongside the water on the New Jersey side, where a limousine awaited their arrival.

Cadence looked at him and shook her head. Blake smiled and waved her into the vehicle. During another short ride, Cadence held his hand. She didn't bother asking any more questions that she knew wouldn't be answered. Instead, she enjoyed the moment and thanked God for sending her such an amazing man.

Finally, they pulled up to a pier where a yacht awaited.

"Oh! We're going on a dinner cruise. I haven't been on one of those in so long."

"Just wait!"

Cadence clapped her hands again in delight. She was enjoying the suspense. When they got on the boat, Blake whispered to a young man, sharply dressed in a blue naval-inspired suit. The young man led them through the boat into a dining area. Cadence looked on with a huge smile, appreciating the effort Blake went through to make this night special. As they were being led to their table, Cadence noticed a group of diners standing. She shook her head and realized she knew almost everyone in the room. She was so caught up in her excitement that she hadn't noticed her father, Alana, Blake's parents, brothers and a host of other friends. Her mouth fell open.

"Surprise!" they all yelled at once.

Cadence turned to Blake to ask what this was all about and he pulled a small box from his pocket and dropped to one knee.

She covered her gasp and tears sprang to the wells of her eyes.

"Cadence Payne, will you marry me?"

Her cries made it difficult to speak. Cadence caught her breath, knelt down in front of Blake, grabbed his face in her hands and buried him in kisses. "Of course I'll marry you!"

Applause burst throughout the room. Cadence found herself affectionately surrounded by the people she loved. Blake helped her to her feet. Her father squeezed her in his burly arms and kissed the top of her head. She was elated to have his blessing. After that, there was a receiving line of family and friends waiting for their chance to congratulate her and see the beautiful ring.

"You were in on this?" Cadence shook her finger at Alana.

Alana laughed. "Welcome to your engagement party! I had to make sure Blake didn't mess this thing up," Alana said and laughed again. "I'm just kidding. He asked me for ideas. I found the place. The transportation was all his idea. The man has friends in high places, you know."

"Let's get this party started," Blake yelled, and music flowed from the speakers. He tore his fiancée away from her adoring friends and led her to the small dance floor. Several couples, including his parents, joined them.

As thy danced, Cadence looked over her shoulder and suddenly stopped moving.

"What's wrong?" Alarm was etched into Blake's face.

Cadence nodded in the direction of what had arrested her attention. When Blake noticed what she had been looking at, he gasped. His brother Drew had his hand wrapped around Alana's fit waist and their bodies were pressed close together as they danced. Drew whispered something in Alana's ear that made her giggle with delight and then she rested her head on his shoulder.

Cadence and Blake looked back at each other in shock and burst out laughing.

"Could it be?" Cadence said.

"You never know," Blake said, holding Cadence closer as he swayed to the music. "All I care about right now is my first dance with my new fiancée."

Cadence lifted on her toes to give her husband-to-be a sensual kiss.

* * * * *

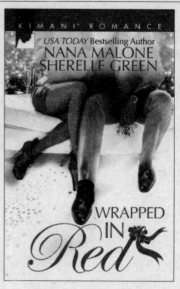

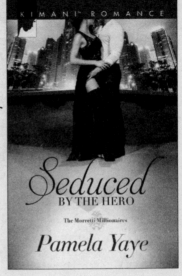

REQUEST YOUR FREE BOOKS!

2 FREE NOVELS
PLUS 2 FREE GIFTS!

KIMANI™ ROMANCE

Love's ultimate destination!

Bailey wondered what there was about Walker that was
different from any other man. All it took was the feel of
his hand on her shoulder... His touch affected her in a
way no man's touch had ever affected her before. How did
he have the ability to breach her inner being and remind
her that she was a woman?

Personal relationships weren't her forte. Most of the
guys in these parts were too afraid of her brothers and
cousins to even think of crossing the line, so she'd only
had one lover in her lifetime. And for her it had been
one and done, and executed more out of curiosity than
anything else. She certainly hadn't been driven by any
type of sexual desire like she felt for Walker.

There was this spike of heat that always rolled in her
stomach whenever she was around him, not to mention
a warmth that would settle in the area between her legs.

Even now, just being in the same vehicle with him was making her breasts tingle. Was she imagining things or had his face inched a little closer to hers?

Suggesting they go for a late-night ride might not have been a good idea, after all. "I'm not perfect," she finally said softly.

"No one is perfect," he responded huskily.

Bailey drew in a sharp breath when he reached up and rubbed a finger across her cheek. She fought back the slow moan that threatened to slip past her lips. His hand on her shoulder had caused internal havoc, and now his fingers on her face were stirring something to life inside her that she'd never felt before.

She needed to bring an end to this madness. The last thing she wanted was for him to get the wrong idea about the reason she'd brought him here. "I didn't bring you out here for this, Walker," she said. "I don't want you getting the wrong idea."

"Okay, what's the right idea?" he asked, leaning in even closer. "Why did you bring me out here?"

Nervously, she licked her lips. He was still rubbing a finger across her cheek. "To apologize."

He lowered his head and took possession of her mouth.

Don't miss
BREAKING BAILEY'S RULES
by New York Times *bestselling author*
Brenda Jackson, available November 2015 wherever
Harlequin® Desire books and ebooks are sold.

www.Harlequin.com